The Mighty Spartan!

And his common man adventures

Edmond P. DeRousse

The Mighty Spartan and His Common Man Adventures
Copyright @ 2015 by Edmond P. DeRousse
All rights reserved

All rights reserved. No part of this book may be reproduced or transmitted in any form or by any means, electronic or mechanical, including photocopying, recording, or by any information storage and retrieval system, without permission in writing from the copyright owner.

This is a work of historic fiction. As a blend of fact and fiction, the names, characters, places, and incidents either are the product of the author's imagination or are references to actual persons, events, and locales, blended within the context of the story, through research.

Library of Congress Control Number: 2015935995
ISBN 13:   Paperback: 978-1-942296-58-4
           PDF: 978-1-942296-60-7
           EPub: 978-1-942296-61-4
           Kindle: 978-1-942296-62-1
           Hardcover: 978-1-942296-59-1

Printed in the United States.

Cover artwork by Wm. Terry Waldron

Praise for
The Mighty Spartan

Pete Russey is The Mighty Spartan, and mighty he is. His life adventures have taken him everywhere exciting, even if it means just in his own backyard! You haven't heard anything yet. He says he's a "common ordinary guy" and his antics are all centered around his small hometown, Sparta, Illinois. The oxymoron here is that Pete's life is BIG with excitement because he lives it in an extraordinary way.

Just call Pete a Mighty Warrior because he's a man defined about who he is... armed with attitude and confidence to tackle whatever comes his way. Whether it's "flying like Superman," "solving the Mona Lisa Smile," "resolving a conflict with an old diary," or confronting the ghost of Mad Myrtle, Pete is fearless. Of course, his ingenuity and a little bit of luck always help too!

There's intrigue and mystery with every turn of the page and Pete is ready for every bit of it. Through it all, like the frightening journey with the motorcycle gang or the battle with the menacing arachnid, Pete is a survivor. On first impression, Pete doesn't come across as exceptional, after all, he claims to be "a common man." But look a little deeper and you see Pierre Jacque Russey, a man of natural talent and exceptional creative ability. Pete has a fighting spirit and he just doesn't give up.

You won't give up either, once you open this book. There's mystery, suspense, humor, and romance-all in one. You're sure to be entertained with Pete's adventures; maybe you'll even reminisce and see yourself as you are transformed into Pete's World. If that happens, just sit back, relax and enjoy the feeling as perhaps your own warrior spirit emerges.

Allow me to introduce you to my friend, Pete Russey-The Mighty Spartan. You deserve the pleasure of meeting him. I'm sure you'll be glad you did. Adventure abounds here. Don't just look at the cover and wonder, "What if?" Open the book, and enjoy the read!

Georgeann S. Henderson, Writer/Journalist

This book certainly captures the feel of our community. The author expresses our values, traditions, and progress with humor and an easy going style. He invites his readers into our community knowing they will identify with something in it. For an insight into what it is like living in Sparta, Illinois, check out **The Mighty Spartan and his common man adventures.**

Charles Kelley, Mayor Sparta, Illinois

I could see myself growing up along with the character in Sparta and could easily identify with much of the book. The chapter about Summerville Woods was particularly fun since I own a farm near there. This was a fun read. I encourage others to read this book.

Best regards, Bob Holloway

This is an enjoyable book to read and full of fun adventures. Although this is fiction, I found myself remembering similar exploits of my own.

Darrel Grathwohl, Retired

The Author has a unique way of writing about ordinary people in an entertaining and personal way.

Latoya Jablonski

Table of Contents

Dedication 1
The Mighty Spartan 3
The Warrior Home 9
Men of Influence 19
O! Christmas tree 25
War Games 33
Summerville Woods 41
The Mona Lisa Smile 51
The Rolling Stones 57
Little Pink Hearts in the Heat of the Night 67
Fowl Owl on the Prowl 75
City Lake 83
The Legend of Mad Myrtle 91
Grandpa Bill 101
Little Warriors 109
Lawful Consequences 117
Arachnophobia 123
Purple Leathers and the Motorcycle Gang 131
Dark and Stormy Night! 141
The Wallet 149
Conflicted 155
City Lake Revisited 161
Asphalt and Mc Donald's 167
Magazine Land U.S.A. 177
Sparta, Illinois USA (My hometown) 183

Dedication

Mayor Kelley left a big hole in the city of Sparta when he passed away in the fall of 2014.

He was a big supporter and promoter of this Mighty Spartan.

Mayor Kelley was a longtime resident and Sparta patriot. He fought and won many battles for our town.

Mayor Kelley. You, my friend, were the true Mighty Spartan.

You are missed.

It is for these reasons and many more that I am dedicating this book to the memory of:

Charles H. "Charlie" Kelley, Mayor
Sparta, Illinois.

The Mighty Spartan

My name is Pierre Jacque Russey. I am known to my friends as Pete. I was born and raised in Sparta, a small town in Southern Illinois. It was then, and still is, a neat little town.

As a youngster, I wondered if the town had any connection to ancient Greece. I remember studying in history class about the continuous battles between the ancient cities of Athens and Sparta. Since I was not aware of a city called Athens anywhere near me, I figured the mighty Spartans conquered the lowly Athenians. That made my little town a very mighty town indeed.

I was only a little kid when I had those thoughts, so I hope you excuse my youthful exuberance. Besides, kids don't need much of a reason to create their own interesting history.

In my young mind, sword yielding warriors portrayed a great example of manliness. So having connections with ancient Greek warriors was cool. They were men with bulging biceps, brandishing swords, protecting themselves and others with cool looking shields, and dressed in armor. And what about those beautiful Greek Goddesses those warriors were always seen around?

I was given a plastic sword and shield for Christmas one year. Instantly I became a great warrior while alternately jabbing and thrusting my sword and shield upon my attackers.

It didn't matter to me that there was eighteen inches of snow on the ground, that the temperature was below zero, or that I was confined by the walls of my house. I had the sole responsibility of protecting my family, my friends, my community, my domain, or die trying.

I am not so sure, though, that my parents thought they did the right thing by giving me the opportunity to save Sparta from the Athenians. I remember Mom telling Dad something about a broken lamp.

I do have a childhood memory of a Greek warrior likeness being displayed on some kind of city sign. But that memory could be wrong. I'm much much older now and tend to create my own romantic childhood memories.

If you check the history of my home town, though, you will not find any association with Greek warriors. Instead you will discover that it was established around the late eighteen twenties. The history says that several families came to Southern Illinois from South Carolina. These families originally came from Ireland and Scotland.

A Presbyterian minister, an Irish immigrant, was one of those who settled here. He established a mission, more people moved in, and our history as a settlement began. Eventually they named themselves Columbus.

But there was a problem. There was another community in Illinois with a similar name. Perhaps because of suspected confusion, a town meeting was held and the name was changed to Sparta.

I have yet to discover why the name "Sparta" was chosen. What I do know though, is that the editor of the town newspaper called "The Columbus Herald" suggested the name Sparta. No one really knows why he chose that name. The name stuck and in 1839 Sparta was chartered.

So much for the romantic notions of the Greek warrior!

The Russeys have a long history in Southern Illinois. My father even convinced his college sweetheart to move away from her beloved home in Pennsylvania and relocate here to raise their future family.

If you were to visit the historic Ft. Kaskaskia National Park and walk through the cemetery, you would find many of the family names on the tombstones. My parents, in fact, insisted my name came from one of those tombstones.

From an early age I believed I would never leave. I think I felt protected by that small town. Kind of like being a sibling in a strong family unit. But, life called me away for a few years to experience adventures outside my home.

After leaving, my intent was always to return to my roots. The journey was long, but with God's help I did manage to make it back home in time to raise my children. I have since retired, and I am still proud to call Southern Illinois and Sparta, in particular, my home.

I like living in Sparta. It is quiet and full of hard working, caring, family centered people. Growing up here, to me, was really like growing up in Mayberry, North Carolina. You know, that fictional community where Sheriff Andy Taylor raised his son Opie. I was told many times, even by strangers, that I reminded them of Opie.

Back in the early seventies, I worked for a short time for the post office at Southern Illinois University in Carbondale. While delivering mail, I was once told by a secretary, without any prompting from me, that I looked like an older Opie.

As a college student, I was not sure how to take that comment. I told her she was not the first to tell me that. At that time in our US history, there certainly could have been less attractive people to be associated with.

The fifties and sixties! What a great era to have lived in and be from! But even Mayberry cannot ignore the onslaught of modern technology.

Life today is much different. It's much more complicated, stressful, and, according to the media, less friendly.

Even Sparta could not totally escape modern day challenges. Yet most of us still know and communicate with our neighbors. And I am not talking about through Face Book. It is not uncommon to sit on each other's porches and talk about the day's events.

I remember sitting on my front porch one afternoon with my wife and some friends watching our neighbor's old vacant double wide trailer being hauled off. The neighbors had not hired professional movers. They were using friends. It took several attempts and several hours with a front loader to squeeze each section on separate trailers.

It was very entertaining, to say the least. I was tempted to film it and submit my video to some kind of reality TV show. My porch partners and I were all quite sure that the sections would break apart during the loading process. But our neighbors persisted and were successful in hauling the sections away. None of us still know how they managed it.

The citizens of my town enjoy life, value family and friends, look for the positive, help each other out, and even go to church together.

If I were to leave my house today and go to Walmart, for instance, I would not have to worry if I forgot to lock my front door. I still don't worry about locking my car while it is in my driveway. When my brother from Houston, Texas visits, I always kid him about locking his car in my driveway.

I consider myself a common ordinary guy and enjoy the life that comes with that status. Life, for me, began in Sparta and when I had to leave, it was important for me to return. I am happy to be home. My heart is here.

I love my little town. I feel secure here. Sparta is where I was born and raised and established my values. It supports me and my family.

When life sent me away, I picked up my shield, brandished my sword and battled with it to return. I plan to die here.

I am, Pete Russey, the mighty Spartan, an ordinary citizen in the small Southern Illinois town of Sparta, Illinois.

I am sure that you will find my adventures, here, entertaining. You will experience frightening journeys, some warm and fuzzies, mysteries, and even romantic encounters. I guarantee that you will get a chuckle or two and, perhaps, even identify with some of it.

In the year 2014 my home town, Sparta, Illinois, celebrated its 175th birthday. It has a long rich history. It has been my experience that it will continue to find ways to survive and thrive.

The Warrior Home

A warrior needs a place to live and train in while growing up. Mine was a large two story house a block from the business district. Seven people lived and trained in that home. My parents, of course, were the head of the household. I lived there with two older sisters, an older brother, and a younger sister. With a family of seven, there had to be plenty of space to contain all that energy.

I didn't really pay a whole lot of attention to the house growing up. My main interest was living. Youth, as we all know, is about everything else.

My parents were both Doctors of Optometry. Mom did not practice, though. She, in addition to raising us children, helped Dad out with the details of running his practice. Dad's office, when I was very young, was in our home. He conceded to Mom's need to be close to her children.

My childhood home sat atop a slight hill. I remember Dad telling me the house was built in the late 1800's. That made it ancient as far as I was concerned, and a warrior's training ground has to have been around forever.

The outside walls were stucco and white. A brown wooden trim separated the first and second story. About every three to four feet and running vertically to the roof line were four inch boards made of the same wood as the trim. The two windows facing the front of the house on the upper story were gabled. At the rear of the house was a screened in porch, also covered with a gabled roof. On the side opposite the rear porch was another porch which extended the full length of the house. That porch was open and covered with a flat roof.

I am quite sure it was the stucco, wooden trim, roof line, and position on top of the hill that gave that old house its distinguished appearance. I know there were many older homes like mine in town and just as distinguished. But that was my home and my memories. It was that home which played a big part in developing my character.

Our warrior home had a spacious back yard enveloped on three sides by bushes. I have no idea what kind of bushes they were but they appeared ten feet tall and rather thick. The back yard was my fortress. Inside the wall of the fortress and at the rear of the enclosed yard was a large brick fireplace with a smokestack.

Although I have no memory of a fire ever burning in it, that smokestack played an important part in my development as a child. It was the fifties and Superman was one of the most popular kid's shows on TV. I remember pretending to be that super hero in our back yard. I would tie a bath towel around my neck. My skinny little child frame would climb up on to the top of that smokestack, stretch my arms and hands skyward, and then jump into a clear blue sky. Funny thing, though, against my will, I always came back down to the ground. Fortunately, landing on my feet. Never being satisfied with just one attempt, I would get back up on top of that smokestack and try again. It's been over five decades and I can still remember thinking, "Superman can fly, why can't I?"

The back yard was a great place to play. Those thick bushes provided the family members, who dared, the opportunity to ambush a passer-by with water balloons in the summer and snowballs in the winter.

Dad scolded me more than once about those antics. I'm pretty sure he secretly was not too angry. He enjoyed telling all his children of the mischief he had gotten into as a child. Water Balloons and snowballs didn't come close to some of the antics in his childhood.

I remember one time, though, that those very same bushes, my walls of protection, provided an enemy a definite advantage.

One spring afternoon, the fortress walls were blooming with color. But on that day, the color was unimportant to me. My presence was required downtown and I was late. The route I took meant I had to pass by my backyard, my fortress. The enemy saw that as a perfect opportunity to attack me. He literally flew out of the bowels of the fortress. His sword punctured my neck.

Ultimately, I did win that battle. I slapped the bee from my neck and he moved no more.

Boy, isn't it funny how our memory can be so selective? I can remember things I did over fifty years ago, but I can't remember where in the world I just left my car keys.

The entryway to my house was magnificent. Between the house and the backyard was our circular drive. It was really more like our own cul de sac. Four giant oak trees were strategically placed around the circumference of the drive. In the middle of that massive sheltered circle was green grass. Dad was a golfer in his younger years. I guess that's why that circled area always looked like a putting green. Those giant trees insured there was always shade, even in the hottest part of the summer.

Outside of the circle drive and in front of the backyard was our large outbuilding. It had two huge doors. Dad would drive thru the door on the right and park his big people mover, a 1955 Buick Roadmaster. I can remember making family trips to see Mom's family in Pennsylvania. There were seven people travelling together in that car and I don't recall being squashed.

Through the other larger door was Dad's real pride and joy, Shanghi. It was his twenty foot wooden cabin cruiser. Dad told me it was equipped with a 225 cu.in. inboard/outboard Oldsmobile Wildcat engine. To tell you the truth, I had no idea if what he said was true. But it sounded impressive. This kid was sure impressed with its size. It might as well have been an ocean liner.

One cold winter day, Dad received a call from the place at Crab Orchard Lake where he stored Shanghi that winter. The man on the other end of the phone told my Dad that his boat was underwater. A Coast Guard Cutter had backed into his stall and sank Shanghi.

The Coast Guard Cutter vessel was not a normal thing at Crab Orchard. It was there to break the ice. The vessel needed a place to dock. Shanghi was not the only private citizen boat sunk that day.

Needless to say, Dad was not a happy boater that day.

As much delight as the house outdoors provided us, the indoors could do the same.

Our dining room was huge. It always reminded me of a room where the king and his queen held court. At least it seemed that way on Sundays, which was the only time we came together as a group.

This rectangular shaped room had a long, long table centered in the room. Mom would sit at one end and Dad would sit at the other. That table had to be long to service the Russey's large family.

The Sunday meal was always my favorite meal. Mom made awesome chicken and dumplings, a delicacy we had every Sunday, and I never tired of it.

The dinner ritual seemed like a scene out of Leave It to Beaver, a popular TV show of the 1950s. Family order was very important in that show.

Mom would place the large pot of chicken and dumplings in front of her. Then grab the ladle and a bowl. She would fill the bowl and pass it to the oldest, who always sat on her right. That bowl would be passed down the table to Dad. We probably had mashed potatoes, vegetables and maybe a salad. I didn't like that stuff as a child; so I can't be certain of the extras.

The right side of the table always got served first. My youngest sister and I sat on the left. After everyone got served, Mom would fill her bowl. That process seemed to take forever.

I was the comic relief. I enjoyed my job. These Sunday meals always gave me the opportunity to try out new material, which I planned on using during the week at school.

Adjacent to the dining room was the kitchen. It was a working room only and not intended for family gatherings. A much smaller round table was in this room. We would assemble there individually or in small groups on an as needed basis. Mom would only allow us to eat snacks at that table or outside.

On Sundays, after the evening meal and the dishes were put away, we would all regroup in the family room. Like the dining room, this room was also large. The ceiling may have been twelve to fifteen feet high.

That living room was the center of many Sunday evening conflicts. Those conflicts were caused by Perry Mason and the Cartwright clan. Mom and the older siblings liked Perry. The younger kids liked the Cartwrights. They both had TV shows on at the same time but different channels. Mom and her supporters usually won out. But the opposition never went down without a fight. Eventually, the opposition managed to defeat the Mason supporters. I think our victories had something to do with the fact that Perry Mason had run out of episodes.

Our house was also the focal point for not only our family but friends of the family as well, especially the older siblings. It seemed like there was always some older boy or girl hanging around.

I guess with five kids, there must have been lots of food. I don't remember Mom or Dad expressing any displeasure about the added mouths.

As a kid, I was not particularly happy about all those older mouths. They ate so much I was concerned there would be nothing left for me. I bet, though, Mom and Dad looked at that situation, as I do now. What a great opportunity to keep an eye on the children!

The 1950s was the start of the "Cold War." That was a term used frequently. As a grade school kid, I didn't really know what it meant. The term "Cold War" was confusing to me. I knew war was bad, but I wondered, "Did the soldiers run around in coats because they were fighting in the Arctic?"

All I knew was that it was supposed to be scary. That was the emotion we were to feel when the teachers would have us practice diving under our desks. I believe they called it "duck and cover." In retrospect, what good was that going to do anyway when the blast did occur?

Dad made sure our house protected us from the perils of the "Cold War." He dug a very large rectangular shaped hole under the house. Dad called this hole our "Bomb Shelter."

Our home had two stories above ground. The purpose of the top floor was sleeping and bathing the kids. There were three large bedrooms and a full bath which had a cast iron bath tub with feet. The top floor also had several walk-in clothes closets. One of them had a front and back entrance.

Only one bedroom had a door and that room belonged to the oldest. It overlooked the circle drive and those huge oak trees. I know this to be true, because I snuck in one day. I really don't remember much else about it. It had a door on it for a reason. The privacy it implied was always strictly enforced by its occupant. By the time it was my turn to inherit the room, we moved to a different house.

Because of the lack of privacy, I spent very little time in the upstairs. My time there was occupied by sleeping, bathing, and changing clothes. Homework for me was done downstairs at the kitchen table. I did not like to be alone up there. Too many places for the scary things to hide in.

Dad would sometimes have to sort out whose fault "it" was. Once the culprit was determined, the guilty would be sent upstairs by him or herself. Often that person was me. My little sister, the youngest, seemed to be better at arguing her case.

My parents raised five children in the homestead. I consider myself very fortunate to have lived the first fourteen years of my life there. The stability and coziness that home provided the family of my youth is something I have always striven for with my own family.

Coziness I provided my family. The stability of being in one place, I could not. My many jobs required me to frequently move.

I only possess one actual photo of that old house. My parents took that picture with the Brownie camera my younger sister and I gave them as an anniversary gift. Both of us saved our money to buy that camera.

Eventually most of the kids moved out of the

house and into lives of their own. Mom and Dad no longer needed all that space. Dad sold it to a local bank. They tore it down and turned the space into a parking lot. The town was experiencing growing pains and it needed the space. For the sake of the town, it gave up its life.

I never told my parents this, but even as a youngster, I recognized the security our family home provided. That house certainly promoted a great example for all of its occupants to strive toward. What a great legacy!

Men of Influence

Every community has them; men, who knowingly or unknowingly, have a positive influence on young lives in their community. I remember those men. For me, they were a neighbor, a school teacher, and local businessmen.

My neighbor, Mr. Smithton, was one of my earliest inspirations. He was a WWII disabled veteran. His legs were paralyzed but he did not use a wheelchair to get around. I think he had one, but I don't remember him using it. There were no ramps in his small house. That impressed me because I thought having paralyzed legs meant being confined to a wheelchair. The Key word here is confined. My neighbor got around, as well as I did, on crutches. Sometimes I had to run to keep up.

Mr. Smithton had a 1947 Pontiac Torpedo in his garage, which he drove. He had his car equipped with hand controls. He and his wife were my Cub Scout leaders. I built my pinewood derby car in his garage and used it as my model.

We talked some about his wartime adventures and how he became disabled. He told me his fighter plane crashed while on a mission. Okinawa, I think. But, I was a small child and not much interested in wartime adventures. He was a nice man and we enjoyed each other's company. Hopefully, he didn't consider himself Mr. Wilson to my Dennis the Menace.

He could have used his paralysis as an excuse to be bitter about his life. There was no bitterness in Mr. Smithton. I learned from him about overcoming challenges.

One day, when I got home from school, my mother told me that Mr. Smithton had died. The funeral would be in a couple of days and his memorial service would be in the funeral home across the street from us.

At about ten years of age, that was my first experience with someone close to me dying. I wanted to go, but my parents said I was too young and they would not let me go. I did not agree with them then, and still don't.

Teachers are, of course, on everybody's list of those who impacted one's life. Every teacher had an influence on me. But it was my seventh grade teacher who without doubt gave direction to my life. Mr. Whiting was that man. He was my home room seventh grade teacher. Because of him, I learned to write.

All his students respected him and respectfully feared him. There were no discipline problems in his classroom. We all knew he had a paddle in his desk drawer. (It was 1963 and paddling was allowed.) He had no need to use it, though.

He had a stare. If you did something wrong and his stare reached you, the thing you did was find the nearest hole, climb into it, and then close it up around you. But it never worked. The stare always found you and you would have to deal with him and his always fair and just discipline. His students found it much easier to not deal with his stare.

Mr. Whiting taught diagramming; a method no longer taught in schools. Because of diagramming, I visually learned parts of speech and every word's purpose. I have always been a visual learner, so mapping out words on a piece of paper made sense to me. Consequently, writing became fun. In fact, I wound up majoring in English in College. The writing skills I developed in his class helped my advancement throughout my various careers.

I don't believe there was a kid in town who did not know Scotty or T.J. They each had a business every kid frequented.

Scotty owned a Dime store. We had two dime stores in Sparta, but his was special. Maybe it was the candy that drew all us kids to his store. It had a variety of Pez dispensers, candy cigarettes, KoolAid in straws, just to name a few. I still remember those display cases full of loose candy. Mine was Bridge Mix.

One could buy candy by the scoop-full back then. Scotty would grab a scoop, open up the candy door of your selection, and then shovel out a bunch of candy. I would watch the candy fall out of the scoop and onto a scale.

It seemed to me as if he always scooped out the correct weight. Scotty never went back for more, nor did he take any out off the scale. He'd just grab a bag from under the counter and let the candy slide out of the scale and into the bag. I'm sure many of us "Old Timers" in town have Scotty to thank for our early fillings.

It was magical in there. Every kid's wants were always there or he could get it. I spent a great deal of time searching through his shelves of model cars and model airplanes. A couple of times I think he even offered to help me put my selection together.

It seemed as if each and every kid who went in his store was Scotty's favorite grandchild. He knew everybody by name and always had time for you.

T.J. was another man of influence. He ran the movie theatre. We only had one so that was where everybody went to view a motion picture. We could have gone to movie houses in towns a few miles away, but back in the sixty's traveling to other communities to see a movie didn't seem as convenient as it does today.

Like most movie theatres of the day, our theatre had the traditional triangular shaped marquee over the entrance. It would announce the current movie and its stars. Inside was a glass enclosed booth with a hole in it from which tickets could be dispensed. It also had a separate counter from which refreshments could be bought.

Many of Sparta's youth had their first employment at the show, and T.J. was their boss.

T.J. collected everyone's ticket with a smile as they entered the amphitheater. After the movie started, he insured everyone behaved. He'd walk up and down the aisles with a flashlight. If misbehaving, he would snap his fingers twice, turn on his flashlight, and shine it on you for all to see. Nothing needed to be said.

Kids would go to the show and sit in packs. The intent was not necessarily to watch the movie. It was a good time to visit with friends, to impress the girlfriend or boyfriend, and perhaps even sneak a kiss or two. Always, though, taking care not to have T.J. shine his flashlight on you. He knew your parents.

T.J. managed the theatre with a firm but fair hand. Whether we admitted it or not, we all were thankful for that. He was never mad and always polite. It was a safe environment. He seemed to really like being around people.

These were men who were truly interested in being good role models. I am quite sure I did not realize it then, but these men certainly made a positive impression on me. But I think, good men are good and don't make a big deal out of it. They lead by example. I know they each had their own adversities to deal with, but fought through them. They were true warriors.

O! Christmas tree

I have many pleasant memories of the family Christmas tree.

Thinking back on it now, my Christmas tree experience seems more like something Norman Rockwell would paint. I grew up in the 50s and have since seen many Rockwell paintings, so perhaps my memories are somewhat tainted by that. But on the other hand, I really do have vivid memories of my childhood. I think Norman Rockwell most likely painted things which reflected my life.

Besides my Mom and Dad, there were five children in my childhood home. I had two older sisters, one older brother and one younger sister. We all took part in decorating the Christmas tree, one way or another.

Christmas was a special time for me. I knew it meant Santa Claus was on his way, but it also meant a trip to the woods with dad.

I was probably five through ten years of age when we would go Christmas tree shopping. That was a very exclusive experience. Only the men of the house could participate. I felt proud to be included in a man adventure.

About two weeks before Christmas, dad would take me and my brother out to the country to pick out our tree. I remember walking with him through the forest of prickly pine trees. Finding our tree wasn't an easy thing to do because the room in which the tree was going had a tall ceiling, probably twelve to fifteen feet in height. At five years of age it seemed a hundred feet tall.

The tree we brought home had to be just right, of course. If it was too small, the living room would look funny with a little tree. It had to be a large, full tree. But, at that age, obviously, I had no concept of largeness. Even the little trees were big to me.

To check the largeness of a tree, I would extend my hand as far as I could above my head and look up. If I couldn't touch the tip of the tree, I thought it was big enough, and if I thought it didn't look puny, I would tell my dad to "Take that one! Take that one!" Dad would usually tell me the one I picked was not the perfect tree we were looking for. He would then reassure me that the perfect tree was still out there. We just had to keep looking.

The weather was always cold and the snow deep. Back in the 50s, that seemed to be more of the norm. Of course, I was a child. I am much older now, so perhaps my memory of that time is a bit gray. We grayer folks tend to remember Southern Illinois winters that way.

Regardless of the weather, dad would never cut down the first tree I selected. We would trudge on until we, he, found the "perfect" tree. Once identified, it was then and only then, that dad would take his saw, not an ax, and start cutting down the gigantic tree.

The first year of the adventure I asked him why he didn't cut it down with the ax I knew he had in the garage. He told me that the "saw cut" made the bottom fit better in the tree stand. I'm a dad now, so I know what he really meant. I wasn't much more than a baby and I couldn't be trusted to be anywhere near that ax.

He used a two man saw, which of course I wanted to be on the other end of. Any young boy would consider that a fun adventure, at least until the fun wore off. Dad would let me try, anyway. He knew it wouldn't take long before I would discover that I couldn't do it and lose interest.

My bigger brother, who was much older, was able to handle the other end of the saw. He would stand back and direct Dad and me while we attempted to fall the "perfect" tree.

My brother would patiently wait until I was satisfied that I couldn't do it and plead for him to take over. He knew, I'm sure, that there would be less of an opportunity for a whine session from me if he waited until I determined the work was too hard.

Once I relinquished the saw to my brother, the real cutting began. My new job, I determined, was to aid them by holding the tree up as they cut. I couldn't understand, though, why they kept telling to me to stand back when I was trying to be so helpful. In my mind I guess I was afraid of our Christmas tree falling on them. And if it did, I probably thought myself strong enough to hold up the falling tree as they scampered out from underneath it.

I can still remember thinking "This must be what it's like to be a lumberjack." I would shout "Timmm—berrr!" as the tree fell to the ground. I was Paul Bunyan, and I knew that was what he yelled.

After the tree was down, we would drag it out to the trailer, tie it down, and head back home. How we got that giant of a tree through the house door I don't remember, but it always came through.

I was probably more of a hindrance than a help. But, Dad and my brother made me feel like I was an important part of the adventure.

Once the tree was in the house, it had to be uprighted. I can't recall how he did it, but Dad somehow got the tree to stand up and then we could start the decorating process which required the use of a tall ladder.

My mom, dad, brother, three sisters and I all got involved with the decorations. It must have been mass congestion in that room with all those people, boxes of decorations, and that massive tree.

Mom took over here. She assigned each of us a special job. Mine was the tinsel. Years later, though, Mom reminded me that some of the tinsel got clumped up on the limbs and she waited until I went to sleep to straighten them out. Mom suspected a loss of interest on my part if she spent too much time trying to correct my clumps. I am sure she was right. Pretending to be Paul Bunyan was definitely more fun than working with the tinsel.

What I liked best, though, about our tree were the bubble lights. There were several strands of them. I know we had twinkle lights, but watching the bubbles was special to me.

I remember staying behind in the room after everyone else left. I would watch the bubbles travel up and down the tube and try to figure out how those bubbles did that. That was my Christmas mystery.

Unfortunately, my children did not have the opportunity to enjoy the bubbles. The world had moved on to other Christmas tree decorations by then.

Dad had one more job to perform on that day.

Mom reached into her special box and carefully unwrapped her favorite ornament. It was a lighted Angel passed down to her from her family. Dad climbed the ladder one last time, gathered up a few of the uppermost limbs, and gently stuffed them into the hole in her bottom. Mom was watching, so dad had to be careful. When I looked at the Angel, I knew she was looking to the heavens and perhaps was even guiding Santa Claus to my house.

Everyone pitched in and the tree was eventually deemed ready to celebrate the Christmas holiday. Even at that young age, I was in awe or our tree. It was not one hundred feet tall but it sure seemed that way to me. It soared and twinkled well above my small stature.

Christmas Eve night was lively. On that night each member of the family would pick out one gift from under the Christmas tree and open it. This routine was particularly tough on the youngest of the brood, because the oldest (Dad) opened first while the rest of us waited. And no other gifts were opened until all had the opportunity to experience that gift.

There were seven gifts to be opened that night. Mine was number six. Mom and Dad always opened theirs with no ceremony. As I remember, my two older sisters followed in the same manner. Not my older brother. The presentation ceremony was just as important to him as what he unwrapped.

Everyone shared in his experience. Each and every one of us, separately. That, of course, added to the anxiousness for me and my younger sister.

After the gift unwrapping was over Mom and Dad would head off to bed. The rest of the family would stay up late into the night watching that tree twinkle.

The oldest siblings would share readings of Christmas stories. Eventually someone would read "T'was the Night Before Christmas!" and some of us would even try to stay up long enough to see that jolly old man in the red suit.

To make that wait easier, Mom had baked a batch of Oatmeal cookies (my favorite). The plan was to share them and a glass of milk with Santa.

All the older siblings, who stayed up, took special delight in convincing the two youngest that we would meet the man in the red suit in person.

My younger sister and I would have to try to convince the older siblings that we were more nice than naughty. Honestly, though, I think mom and dad put them up to that particular interrogation.

Even though I waited up to see Santa, I was still fascinated by those bubble lights.

How did they actually bubble? Water, as far as I knew, only bubbled when it boiled. I knew the water inside the bulb was not hot enough to boil water. It took time to heat water to that temperature. But those things bubbled as soon as the tree was switched on. Perhaps I thought I could ask Santa Claus when I saw him.

Presents from Santa Claus were never under the tree on Christmas Eve night. He was supposed to bring them sometime during the night after everyone was asleep. That's what we were told, which may explain why we never saw him. We had to be asleep. As long as we stayed up he wasn't going to come.

I remember the year I believed it was no longer cool to believe in Santa Claus. I don't think I told Mom and Dad that I no longer believed, but I must have thrown out plenty of hints. The problem was Mom and Dad were not ready for me to give up on believing in Santa's existence.

An exception to our Christmas Eve tradition happened that year I gave up on Santa. There was a present under the tree from Santa with my name on it. When my turn came to open a present, I was directed to open it instead of one from Mom and Dad.

"Santa brought this especially for you to open tonight" Mom told me. "He heard that you no longer believe in him. He told me it would be a box of air unless you believed in Santa Claus."

She looked me in the eyes and asked, "Do you believe in Santa Claus?"

I was probably eight or nine at the time and I was

sure there would be more presents from Santa under the tree on Christmas Day. You better believe I told Mom that I still believed. I wonder how those Christmas day gifts from Santa with my name on them would have been explained away if I had said "no."

In all those years of waiting, I never did see Santa Claus.

I would be hard pressed to say which Christmas tree adventure I miss the most. Cutting the tree down and decorating it or staying up late with my siblings telling Christmas stories and waiting on Santa.

The last few years we lived in that house a new phenomenon took over. It was the artificial tree. The trips to the Christmas tree forest with my dad were over.

I did not continue the natural tree tradition my father had begun. I had succumbed to the artificial Christmas tree phenomenon by the time my son came along. My wife and I did enjoy, though, decorating our unnatural tree with our own children. We both managed to save a couple of decorations from our parent's family trees.

We shared those memories with our children and now with grand children.

The new Christmas tree tradition is different now, but it is still special.

War Games

I was ten years old in 1960. The world, then, was facing a period of heightened international tension and competition.

That's what everyone was told to believe.

International tension and competition? I had no idea what that meant. The only world I knew about was what I could see in front of me. And that's all that was important to me and to most kids my age.

It was John Wayne, cowboys and Indians, the neighbor kids, and my school buddies. It was riding bikes, and building forts. It was swimming in the community pool, and playing little league ball. It was Roy Rogers, Sky King, and Saturday morning serials.

The adults felt nervous. They tried to hide it. There were signs that told us they were nervous, if we paid attention. They tried not to pass it on to us. But deep down, we could tell something was wrong. They didn't talk about it at home. Yet they prepared us for it.

We were given some facts about it in the guise of an educational atmosphere. Fear of it caused teachers to teach us how to take cover. So we practiced hiding under our school desks. The faster the better. Whatever we were doing had to be stopped at that exact instant. No delay. Delay would be deadly. Something about a blinding light, a mushroom cloud, and a gigantic wave of energy.

Funny thing, though, I can only remember being told to take cover under my desk. What if that blinding light happened while I was out on the playground?

Thinking back on that light and gigantic energy wave now, I guess that meant that stuff was only going to happen when we were in our classrooms. Those guys who made the blinding light happen must have been geniuses in order to time its appearance in such a way.

What is "It?" you ask? There was a name for all that worldly tension. "They" called it the "Cold War."

"Cold War?" That was a peculiar name. A ten year old doesn't understand things the way adults do. When I heard that term back then, I envisioned men fighting in Canada or some other place very cold. I was vaguely aware that some big war had recently ended. A lot of countries were involved. My neighbor, who walked around on crutches, said the plane he flew was shot down in some place he called Korea.

It was during that "Cold War" time that my neighbor shared his war story with me. I don't remember too much anymore about how it happened. He really didn't share that much about it because he probably thought I was too young to understand the severity of his difficult situation. Or perhaps he thought a real life story like that should have come from my parents.

I do remember him saying something about strafing the ground. On his final mission, he said a stray bullet fired at him from the ground somehow disabled his jet. He flew an F-4 Corsair. The bad guy's lucky shot hit the part of his plane which controlled landing. Because of that he didn't have enough control of his plane to land it on the aircraft carrier without crashing. As a result of the crash he broke some vertrabrae in his back. He never made a big deal out of it. My neighbor was a real live hero to me.

WWII, the war to end all wars, was over. So was the skirmish, as some people called it, in Korea. That conflict between democracy and the spread of communism ended in a stalemate. The same conflict, though, was now developing in Southeast Asia.

Fortunately, all that conflict occurred on foreign soil. But by the sixties, America was beginning to worry it would have to defend its own turf. Many were convinced Communism, Russia in particular, was about to attack America. We had to be prepared to defend our own soil. The cost was most likely going to be great. We were led to believe most people on Earth were going to die,

Atomic bombs were dropped on Japan in 1945 by the US. Russia had the same technology except that both the US and Russia by 1960 could now land those bombs on each other's country mounted on guided missiles. Each country told the other that they would send them over if they felt the need to defend territory. Each country had more guided missiles than required to totally destroy each other's country.

"What would be the THING to happen which would require the US and Russia to defend its territory by use of missile?" "Who would be the first to push the button?" "How much of the earth would actually survive the nuclear holocaust?" These were questions on every American citizen's mind.

We all learned about nuclear fallout; the result of radioactive dust which was created when nuclear weapons detonated. The explosion created a massive fireball, possibly several miles wide. Everything within it vaporized. The stuff inside the cloud would turn to dust and that dust became radioactive. If you weren't on ground zero, which was certain death, the dust most likely would kill you.

The US government felt responsible for responding to heightened public anxiety. The Federal government distributed information to instruct the public on how to protect itself in case of a nuclear attack. The thinking was, its citizen could survive an atomic bomb and consequently avoid wholesale death and destruction such as occurred on the scale of Hiroshima.

The School also did its part to try to train all the kids on how to prepare for the inevitable. That horrible stuff could happen at any moment. That evil country, they told us, was Russia. It may drop a bomb on us and then we would have to drop our bombs on them. Thus the total annihilation of the world.

I seem to remember thinking there were a couple of guys in military uniforms working for the good guys and the bad guys, each sitting in a chair, hand hovering over a big red button, and waiting for the order to push it. Once pushed that would be the end of everything. Then nothing would matter anymore.

To add to the adult tensions, square yellow signs with yellow and gray triangles painted inside them started appearing around town. The signs were posted outside what was called a fallout shelter. We were told the places where they appeared were safe places to go when that bright light and gigantic energy wave showed up. Those places were mostly in schools and some public places.

My dad had a shelter built at our house. It, like much of the country, had also fallen prey to the fears of that "Cold War."

Dad hired a bunch of men to dig a large rectangular hole under the house. It was deep, wide and long. I bet I could have stood on my Dad's shoulder and still not see out of the hole. I thought he was building some kind of underground fort. He said he was in a way.

After the hole was dug, twelve inch thick concrete walls were poured around the hole. The entrance to the hole was through the basement. That entrance, I remember was gray in color and looked very heavy. Kind of like a bank vault door. Supposedly, the intent was to withstand the gamma rays emanating from the bomb.

I didn't understand what gamma rays were, but they sure sounded scary. After Dad tried to describe them, I had visions of my skin falling off my body and my eyes plopping out of my head. Dad didn't tell me that. My imagination took a few liberties. So if Dad said it was time to go to the fallout shelter, you bet I would go there without hesitation.

The shelter was also stocked with several months of nonperishable foods. An emergency air and lighting system was installed. Those systems and the food would sustain our family in that shelter for several months. Dad made sure the proper air filter which detected poison outside air was in working order.

Being forced to stay within the confines of those four walls, for who knows how long, was terrifying. If the bomb dropped and Dad sent his family to the shelter, meant I was going to be living in very close quarters with my family. I didn't like my little sister very much back then. That obviously was a bigger problem than the reason we were in there in the first place. So an escape plan was necessary.

Escape, of course, meant running the risk of experiencing my skin falling off and my eyes plopping out. And, somehow, I had to accomplish "the great escape" without the knowledge of my always vigilant parents.

Or perhaps it would have been worse being cooped up in that small room with my entire family because all escape attempts would ultimately fail. I knew any family member at any given time and without a good reason as far as I was concerned was going to have a tirade. It would only be a matter of time. That would be really unpleasant too. Especially if it was my youngest sister who had the tirade.

After it was built, though, the only time I was in it was the day after Dad deemed it completed and the day, years later, we threw all the stuff in it away.

I never ever explored that room. What that room implied was just too scary. Besides, if I did decide to explore the room without anyone knowing, that bank vault door might accidentally close behind me sealing me in it forever. Never mind the fact that Dad had the ability to get me out as soon as he knew I was there.

Yet, for me, I wasn't really concerned about the so called Cold War. There was no war going on around me. At least not one that I could see.

Well. That wasn't exactly true. I and my neighbor, Bill, were most likely at war with bank robbers and practicing our dying moves. Sometimes we thought we could have won Oscars for our portrayals of death scenes. Actually, they would have been the Rotten Tomato award. Kids' wars, as you know, are not very realistic.

We never gave it any thought how many times we could shoot our six guns without reloading, or how many times or how many different places in the yard we could die. Or how many times the other guy could be standing a couple of feet in front of you and shoot you in the chest and hear these words "Ya missed me!"

When we got tired of fighting bank robbers, we would change our pretend cowboy costumes for Calvary uniforms and go after Geronimo or Sitting Bull or some evil band of Indians. That exercise required the participation of a few more people, though. So we would have to recruit more soldiers. In our minds, Indians always seemed too far outnumber the Calvary.

Bill and I were very seldom Indians. Drawing a six gun out of a holster or grabbing a rifle off a pretend horse was a lot cooler looking than shooting a bow and arrow. Besides it took too long to put that arrow in the bow and then let it fly. Cowboys and Calvary officers also had cool hats. Indians had those feathers.

I was too busy clearing the West of the bad elements to be much aware of the tensions felt by my parents and the other adults around me. But I am also sure my childhood must have unconsciously become extremely important. Yet with all that scary stuff being presented to the world, I don't really remember feeling scared. I was just too busy being a kid. Besides my kind of war was much more fun and my buddy, Bill, and I were pretty sure we would never actually see a real dead person.

Summerville Woods

I believe life was simpler when I was a kid. Computers, cell phones, or x-box games, were not needed to have fun. The great outdoors could provide plenty of that.

One of the summertime activities of many young men was camping. Yes, girls and cars were important. This adventure will include both those pastimes. How could any kind of a story about teen age boys not include girls and cars?

Two or three miles to the south of town was Summerville Woods. It was a haven for those of us who liked to camp. I have no idea who owned the woods. Whoever did had to know it was a frequent camping spot. We always pitched our tents in the same location every time we went to the woods. It was on top of a hill and overlooked a rock road.

These campouts would usually take place on a Friday night. Saturday was reserved for cruising around with our girlfriends.

Most of us would arrive at the campsite around 4:00 to 5:00 p.m. Someone would build a campfire for cooking. Each of us brought our own supper to cook. These suppers would vary from hot dogs to marinated steaks.

In the summer of 1967 shortly after 4th of July I decided to pack my tent and head out to Summerville Woods with several of my friends.

My meal on this night was carefully chosen. It had to be easy to cook. I was going to barbeque a hamburger. (Pay attention to my meal selection. It will prove very valuable later in the story.) The night turned out to be the most memorable night I have ever had.

This was the first time John Smith had ever been camping. He had heard about our infamous campouts.

We never cared who camped with us. We only had one condition and that was all first time campers had to go Snipe hunting with us. Snipe hunting was a ritual and its secrets were not to be shared. John had agreed to the hunt.

Anyone who has ever been Snipe hunting knows it cannot happen until it is completely dark. Snipes are nocturnal creatures. They are also extremely rare. Because of their rarity, it would be highly unlikely that John would actually catch one. John was a competitor and accustomed to winning. This was shaping up to be a really great night.

In Southern Illinois in July the dark of night would come late. My friends and I had all the equipment ready for the night's activity. In our part of the world, Snipe hunting required a burlap bag, a walking stick, a rope, and the all important Snipe food.

The burlap bag was used to hold the captured Snipe. The walking stick was used to chase the Snipe out of its hiding place and for protection if needed. Of course, the food was used for enticement.

There have been reports of Snipes attacking people. So you have to be careful how you hunt them. We told John that our group was considered by many in the community to be the experts on hunting these creatures. John knew he could trust us. He couldn't wait to get started.

About two hours after supper, someone said he thought he heard a Snipe. It was time to go hunting. The group gathered up John and the equipment and headed down the hill into the woods. I stayed at the campsite. Someone had to chase the Snipe back down into the woods if it stumbled into the campsite.

A half hour went by and suddenly I heard a blood

curdling scream. The hair stood up on the back of my neck. I didn't know what had happened. I had to stay put, someone might need me.

Bill and Jackson came laughing into the campsite. I was confused. Then they asked me if I still had any of my barbeque sauce left. I told them I did. Apparently they had forgotten to inform me about how they changed the hunt. The sauce was for the fake blood to use on Jackson. They decided to pretend Jackson got bit by the Snipe. Thus the scream. I liked the impromptu addition. Jackson applied the sauce to his leg and the two of them headed down the hill back into the woods.

A few minutes later the group walked into the camp carrying Jackson. John appeared to be ghostly white. I'm sure it was a combination of the excitement of the hunt and concern for his fellow hunter. Jackson was moaning and Bill had the burlap bag over his shoulder. Jackson was brought over to me. I had the 1st aid kit. I attended to Jackson's pretend wound while the rest of the group took turns patting John on the back.

You see, he was a great hunter. He captured an elusive Snipe. It was in the bag.

John wanted to see it, but we convinced him that if he opened the bag at night it would wake up and escape. We all told John he had to wait until the morning light to open the bag.

What a great night. But it was just beginning…

It was probably around 11:00 p.m. now. We weren't quite ready to turn in for the night and so we just sat around the campfire talking. We watched a car head down the road and stop at the bottom of the hill. The guy in the car gets out. He's singing or at least it sounds like it. Can't really understand him and he is loud. We think he's drunk and hope he doesn't know we're up here on the hill. We think there might be a girl in the car with him.

Suddenly, Bill walks to the edge of our campsite and starts having a conversation with that guy. We all thought Bill was nuts. The more those two talked the more evident it became Bill was talking to a drunk. We didn't like the fact that a drunk man now knew where we were. We did everything we could to make Bill stop his bantering with the drunk man. But Bill was having too much fun.

The man seemed to be getting angry with Bill. The drunk started walking up our path. Apparently, the man was too drunk to negotiate the path up the hill to our campsite. He stumbled and rolled back down the hill. I thought I saw him take something out of a bag and say something to it. Of that I can't be sure. It was getting too late. None of us were anxious to have him become part of our outing. Fortunately, it didn't matter anymore. He stumbled back into his car and slowly drove away.

If the Snipe hunt didn't get us wound up, this drunken episode was sure to keep us up for a while longer. Especially Bill. I don't know what got into him, but he was just about to lead us into another adventure. And it is now midnight.

Bill was so charged up by now he took control of the rest of the night's activities. He told us the drunk's car looked like Jason Parker's car and that must have been his girlfriend with him. Bill suddenly acted concerned about Jason Parker's safety. He suggested we climb down the hill, follow the road for a while, and make sure Jason and his girlfriend didn't wind up in a ditch someplace.

I was pretty gullible and naïve then. Later that night, I realized Bill's intent was not what he implied.

Anyway, we headed down the road. I reminded Bill that we didn't have our flashlights. He said we didn't need them. As long as we stayed on the road we would be just fine. How odd? Why are we on a rescue mission without flashlights?

About a mile down the road we came upon a car. As we got closer to the car, it appeared to be rocking. Bill told us to go into the bushes opposite the car and stay there until he called us. This was getting weird.

Jackson was with me on the side of the road and reminded me of something I had forgotten. Bill and Jason had a history. They didn't like each other. Bill was sure that Jason stole his girlfriend, Mary.

Bill now had an opportunity to find out if it was true. The car was really rocking now. Bill had managed to sneak up to the rear of the car undetected. He stayed there a few seconds. Suddenly Jackson and I saw a flash and heard a loud B A N G.

None of us realized it, but Bill had a stash of firecrackers and he discharged one at the rear end of that car. (Did you forget the time of year this adventure is taking place?) Whoever was in that car must have been scared to death. Bill ran across the road and told us to not move a muscle until that car left.

I need to let you know something here; Parker was parking with Rosie, his new girlfriend. Parker was the school bully. And Bill just threw a lit firecracker at him.

After what seemed like minutes, Jason Parker opened the car door and headed across the road toward us. He had a club in his hand, and he was naked as a jaybird. You bet I stayed still. He was beating the ground with that club. We must have done a good job hiding because no one got clobbered with that bat.

Parker threw something and it landed near me. He

got back in his car. It was a few more minutes before he drove away. Now we were absolutely convinced we had a problem. That was the school bully and he knew where we were camping. He had friends and wasn't afraid to use them.

We headed back to camp to prepare for our slaughter.

Obviously, we weren't in a great big hurry to accommodate Parker and his friends, so we took our time. We also knew we didn't want to get surprised out here on the road. This was a dilemma. It definitely required strategy.

Lots of ideas were emerging as we made headway back to the campsite. We were so engrossed in developing plans that we almost didn't see the light coming toward us.

At first we weren't sure what we were seeing. Bill told us to stop for a minute. Yep! It was a pair of headlights.

Oh! No! It looked like two or three pair of head lights. We needed to get out of sight in a hurry. We ran into the open field adjacent to the road and hunkered down. When the cars safely passed we got back on the road and continued our journey to slaughter.

A few yards down the road we heard something in the woods. What now? I don't know how much more excitement I can take. The night was pitch black. We all hunkered down to listen. We certainly were caught in a bad spot. The open field was on one side of us and the woods were on the other.

Whatever we heard in the woods sounded human.

We weren't about to move until we knew what we were up against.

We heard footsteps cross the road a few feet in

front of us and walk into the open field. Maybe it would leave us alone?... But it didn't.

That thing just kept walking up and down the field parallel to us. It was really late. Possibly early morning now. We were too tired to be scared.

Bill finally came up with a brilliant idea. He decided he would slither up a few feet, stand up, and yell. When that thing came out to attack him the rest of us would jump on the attacker and beat it off. Sounded like a good plan to us, especially since Bill volunteered to be the attackee.

The plan worked like a charm. Bill stepped forward and screamed like a Banshee. We were ready and primed. But nothing happened. Nothing came out of the field to attack us. We waited for a sneak attack. Still nothing happened. The footsteps ceased.

We all heard those footsteps walk through the woods, cross the road a few steps ahead of us and walk up and down that open field. We never saw anything but we all heard S O M E T H I N G.

I cannot for certainty say ghosts do exist, but I cannot for certainty say they do not exists either. To this day I can still occasionally hear those footsteps. I never did find out what it was. I have heard some speculation, but nothing tangent.

We finally made it back to our campsite. We totally expected company. The place was deserted and nothing was disturbed.

It took us awhile to regain our composure. Once we did we went to sleep, woke up in the morning sunshine, fixed our breakfast, packed our gear and left for home. By the way, I never heard from Jason Parker. I am not convinced he was the man in Summerville Woods that night.

John finally did open up his burlap bag to see his prized Snipe. After the night we just experienced he wasn't a bit surprised to find a log in the bag.

It was a most enjoyable night, indeed. And one I will never forget.

The Mona Lisa Smile

When I was a teenager my parents took me and my sister to Germany for a summer vacation. Mom and Dad included a side trip to Paris, France. While there they drug us to a museum known the world over as the Louvre. Visiting a museum in Paris was not necessarily what I would have considered a favorite thing to do. I much preferred to see some pretty girls.

We were in Paris, France, after all. The city of romance! I was a teenager. Any French girl had a certain allure for teenage boys. Naturally, I had it in my mind to see an alluring French girl, first hand.

But Mom and Dad were dragging me to a museum. And with my sister!

It turned out alright, though. I saw plenty of French beauty at the Louvre. I'm not talking about the art work either. That made the museum visit worthwhile.

One famous work of art Mom and Dad wanted to see was one I remembered from a grade school history book. It was the Mona Lisa. Seeing it, though, caused me a great deal of consternation, weeks later.

We had been in many rooms in the Louvre looking at exhibits. Things flowed pretty well. But, when we finally got to the Mona Lisa room, it was wall to wall people.

We could barely get close enough to see the famous smile.

There must have been a hundred people ahead of us stuffed in that small room. But because we were part of a tourist group, we were on a strict time schedule so we couldn't wait in line to get close enough. That famous smile was seen from afar and through a mountain of heads.

That painting was not such a big deal to me anyway. I wondered why so many people would wait so long to get up close and personal with a painting on a wall.

Me, I preferred looking at the short skirts and tight fitting blouses on all those pretty and very much alive French girls. That was the art worth looking at.

Two months after we got home a new school year had started. I had lots of stories to tell, obviously. My friends were most interested in my interpretation of the French art I saw. And I enjoyed interpreting.

As luck would have it, my teacher found a way to ruin my visit to Paris. She decided her class needed to write an essay on an eternal question. What's behind the Mona Lisa smile?

I wondered if that topic was chosen because she knew of my visit to the famous museum. Or was it just a coincidence?

I saw the smile, sort of, in person. I remember thinking, "What's the big deal anyway?"

Even though I saw the actual painting, that essay still required me to research. As a student, I avoided that type of study, if I could. I did not care about painters. I preferred to study a good action warrior. Action was easier for me to relate to.

Enjoying the outdoors was something I also related well too. It did not matter whether the snow was falling or the sun shining hot. I loved the great outdoors. BUT writing an essay meant I had to spend many evenings visiting the local library to research the topic.

Keep in mind, research in the mid 1960s meant touching and feeling paper. Computers were not something used by a library patron back then.

First of all, a researcher would have to leave the home and somehow get to a building which housed lots and lots of books. After arriving at this building, most likely the researcher would walk to the encyclopedia section and thumb through pages and pages of those reference books for anything that remotely resembled the topic.

Notes would be written on pieces of paper. The books would then have to be returned to shelves which, of course, meant getting up out of your comfortable chair and walk them back over to the shelves they came from.

Usually, encyclopedias did not contain all the answers required for the topic. So researching the card catalog was the next step. More physical effort was expended. (I had nothing against expending physical effort; I just wanted to expend my effort outdoors.)

One had to leaf through a set of boxes containing alphabetized index cards by topic, author, and/or book title. Not an easy chore to quickly accomplish. What if you did not know the author or the title of the book?

Several books had to be identified as possible resources. Those books were found in various locations throughout the library. More physical activity. Then the books had to be pulled from the shelf and then leafed through to find your topic.

Many times books pulled from the shelf only contained a paragraph or two about your topic and was of no value. More notes from these different sources had to be written down on paper.

Of course, all this research had to be done after school. I was never the best of students, so I usually had to spend several nights indoors.

To me it seemed to be poor planning on the part of the teacher who was requiring the research. He or she wanted the paper to be completed on a day after an extended period of beautiful weather. That meant I

The Mighty Spartan! And His Common Man Adventures

was inside wishing I was outside enjoying any kind of outdoor activity.

That, in my opinion, was not fair. How was I supposed to concentrate on research? Why could they not plan for their students to do research on lousy weather days?

Whether I thought the teacher was fair or not did not matter. I still had research to do and an essay to write.

Fortunately, Mona Lisa had much history. That was both an advantage and disadvantage. It was easy to find material to use in an essay. Unfortunately, that meant lots of books to look through, which equated to lots of time being spent indoors in the evenings in beautiful Southern Illinois.

And today's kids think they have it tuff researching on their tablets in the park under a tree?

My extensive research discovered that history does not agree on what's behind the smile on Mona Lisa's face or who the model really was. Some say she was 24 year old Lisa Gherardini, the third wife of a silk merchant, and pregnant.

With research there must be a conclusion, and this was mine. I thought long and hard about that, so pay attention. It's extremely deep.

If, indeed Lisa Gherardini was pregnant, perhaps she was unable to hide her enthusiasm about the new life she was bringing into her old world. Could that be the reason for what appears to be a smile?

I didn't stop there, though, because I had uncovered something I thought strange and worthy of a bit more research. I discovered others believed there was a perverse secret behind her smile. In fact, these people did not believe Mona Lisa was smiling. Instead, she was smirking.

They thought Mona Lisa was really a man. That man was Leonardo da Vinci, the artist himself. They believed he was a cross dresser and he was painting a self portrait.

If that was so, I guess the smirk was appropriate. To be honest, as a teenager, that ended any question I had about what was behind the famous smile.

Needless to say, whether smile or smirk, I am quite sure, the real reason for it died with Leonardo and whoever the real model was.

As for me, I never was an art connoisseur. That is a mystery I do not plan to spend any more time solving. I seriously doubt, anyway, if the question my essay addressed has yet been solved.

But it is neat to say I saw the Mona Lisa in Paris, France in the Louvre.

By the way, Mrs. Franklin, my English teacher, gave me a B+.

The Rolling Stones

Before I retired, I taught GED in a correctional facility to young men who committed a crime. That crime placed them in prison. But sometimes I think I could have been a student in some kind of prison. This is my story to verify that statement, and I am to this day, still sticking to it.

In 1968, in my last year of high school, I probably enjoyed Halloween a bit too much.

My friends and I had planned to turn Halloween into an extended weekend. The end of October in Southern Illinois can be cold. Sometimes extremely cold. But, the weather that year was pretty pleasant. Most of my friends and I were not the type to get into trouble. We generally worked hard to stay out of it. But sometimes things just happen beyond one's control.

My friends, Bill, Jackson, and Ed decided the best way to stay out of trouble on a Halloween weekend was to spend the weekend on Ed's farm. He had horses and lots of land to ride them on. We decided to pack some camping gear with us just in case it got late. This was going to be a terrific weekend. We were all excited.

Thursday before our weekend was to begin Ed and I were going to do some last minute preparations for the next day's ride. We met at my house and by 9:30 p.m. all was planned.

Mr. Tony's malt shop was next door. He made the best milk shakes in town. Getting a shake would be a great way to end the evening. But we never made it to Tony's.

Ed just couldn't help it. Unbeknownst to me, he came prepared for a little Halloween fun.

Ed produced a bar of paraffin (wax to you youngsters). That's when he told me what he really planned to do. He wanted to wax some windows and he intended me to help.

I'm not one who looks for trouble. You see, I was born with a giant X plastered on my back. It might as well be a target. If you and I were to do something wrong, I would be the one to get caught, while you go free, unobserved. With this caper and my luck, I would get caught with wax in hand and Ed would never be observed doing the dirty deed.

Ed said, "We aren't going to wax house windows. It's too easy to get caught. We're going to wax the windows of the cars at the Ford Dealer. No one is ever there at night. The chances of getting caught are a lot less."

Ed was always a persuasive guy. I conceded. By the time we were done, every single window on every single car was defaced with our mighty bars of paraffin. Now, we had a story that we could possibly share with our buddies. You know, stories are important to young men. At that age these kinds of stories are like rites of passage. We believed that we probably even outdid them. And no property was damaged in the process.

We both knew waxing car windows was nothing compared to what others would claim and perhaps do. Ed and I listened to many stories the next day. We decided to stay silent. Each of us for a different reason.

While listening to our buddies tell their adventure, I suddenly remembered something. The car dealership we visited the night before was owned by the father of someone Ed disliked, Jason Parker.

Guess who met us in the parking lot after school. You guessed it. Jason Parker. He was the school's number one bully. And he was standing by Ed's car.

"My pop said he saw you waxing car windows at his lot last night." (He was looking only at Ed.) I was thankful just then that Jason didn't seem to be acknowledging me. "He said if he ever sees you again near his cars he and his shotgun will be waiting."

Ed made some pretty feeble excuse. I, on the other hand, was hoping that Jason couldn't see my knees trembling.

I never bought a car from Parker Ford as long as Mr. Parker owned the dealership. All I could see, whenever I passed it, was Mr. Parker and his shotgun. In reality, I bet he probably never even owned one.

Mr. Parker was always cordial. Jason, on the other hand, earned a bad boy rep with his special knack for oratory and his big bulky physic.

The Halloween weekend was just getting started.

I got in Ed's car after Jason finally allowed us in it. Inside the safe confines of the car we both exhaled, and without saying a word, we left the parking lot, and headed for our destination. Ed and I were going to meet up with Bill and Jackson at my house that day after school. My house always seemed to be the meeting place. I guess it had something to do with a well stocked refrigerator.

Bill had the biggest car. So the plan was for all of us to pile into his big 1966 four door green Plymouth Fury III. It wasn't the super stocked car most of the hot shot guys were driving. But hey! it more than met our needs.

When everyone arrived and had their fill of Mom's refrigerator, we loaded up Bill's car and headed for Ed's farm.

Ed lived way out in the country. The farm bordered a state park.

We would have to drive down the county blacktop a few miles before reaching his lane. It would take us about ten minutes to get there.

We were almost at Ed's lane when we saw a car parked on the side of the road and some guy walking toward us. He was carrying what looked to be a briefcase in his hand and wearing a nice business suit.

I'm sure he had some kind of mechanical problem, but we were in a hurry to start the weekend. Ed's lane was just in sight. So we decided to drive on by.

Bill slowed down to make the turn. I do not know where it came from. But Ed produced a pumpkin. It was Halloween, after all. Perhaps he intended to give it to his parents. His mother made awesome pumpkin pie.

Anyway, he rolled the window down. The next thing I saw was the pumpkin flying out of the window. I'm sure Ed didn't think about the consequences as he chucked it out just as we were passing that fellow. The pumpkin hit that poor guy square in the chest. His arms went skyward, as did his briefcase. The briefcase opened and papers flew out. The guy tumbled backwards flipping him head over heels.

Ed's eyes got as big as silver dollars. Obviously, there was no intent to hit the man. We all made Bill stop the car to see if we could help the guy.

Bill stopped and backed up. You will not believe what happened next. The young man picked himself up and ran as fast as he could into the nearby woods.

Jackson picked up the papers and stuffed them into the briefcase. Bill, Ed, and I went after the man. We wanted to make sure he was OK. We looked for him for the next couple of hours, to no avail.

The weekend activity would have to wait a little while longer. After Jackson said a short prayer for the stranger, we loaded up Bill's car again, turned it around, and headed back to town to report what just happened.

This incident turned out to be a fortunate thing... for the town. You see, a local bank clerk had stolen some valuable papers from the town's only bank. He was on his way to palm them off when he ran across these four teenagers.

Teenagers are not in the habit of reading the back section of newspapers, but we all looked in the next week's Obituaries to see if a man was "killed by a flying pumpkin." You can imagine how relieved we were when the sheriff told us we were not true criminals.

Although we had a part in the apprehension of the real criminal, the Police Chief was not recognizing us as town heroes. After all, that pumpkin did fly out of a moving vehicle in the direction of a pedestrian. It could have been really bad for us, so we were thankful for just getting off with a warning.

We left the police station with a heavy heart and headed for Ed's farm. By the time we got there, it was very late. We just went to bed. But it was a restless night for all of us.

On that Halloween night in 1968, our testosterone was running rampid. As a result of all that happened because of the pumpkin incident, we had convinced ourselves that the criminal knew where we were that night and he was coming after us. We survived the night, though, to live another adventure.

By the way, the criminal was apprehended a month later by local law enforcement.

The next morning, Ed's mom fixed us a hearty breakfast, listened to our story about the previous day's adventure, and then sent us off to saddle up.

Ed led the way to his barn. We saddled the horses and off we went.

Riding horses in the fall is probably the time to

do it, at least for me. The cool air. The heat from the horse. It's enough to warm the body but not enough to encourage sweating. I'm sure as a teenager I did not care much about the beauty of nature surrounding me. But, I remember I just felt different (more at ease) on horseback that time of year.

We rode all day and even tried to do a little bull roping. Those poor cows didn't have a chance. (Yes they were cows, not bulls.) I felt as close to being an authentic cowboy as I was ever going to feel. The brand new boots and cowboy hat, I'm sure, did their part in enhancing my western frame of mind.

Around 5:00 p.m. it was getting dark and it was time to find our place to camp for the night. Ed already knew where it would be.

Remember, I said Ed's farm bordered on a state park. Ed decided we would camp on a cliff overlooking that park. The local Boy Scout troop would be camping in that park below us next to the lake the Government built there.

Ed knew about the scout's campout. He didn't bother to volunteer that information until we set up our own camp. That was OK, though. We knew some of the boys and thought that later we might try to visit with them.

I think we felt like real cowboys up there on that ridge sitting around the campfire, eating the meal we just prepared. I guess we were expecting Clint Eastwood, as Rowdy, to come moseying in from his watch over the herd. "Head 'em up, move 'em out, Rawhide!" It was really peaceful and we needed some peace and quiet after what we had been through the last couple of days.

But, of course, Ed had other ideas. This setting was perfect for him.

Unbeknownst to us, Ed had preplanned this Halloween adventure. He was the practical joker. We knew this and were always in a constant state of vigilance around him. If he was going to pull one off, there was absolutely no way to prepare. The good thing, though, was his practical jokes were always harmless. No one ever got hurt.

Ed built the fire pit about fifty feet from the edge of the cliff and behind a couple of big boulders. He told us the boulders would do a great job of reflecting the heat from the fire back to us while we slept. Sure sounded logical to me.

I knew the Scouts below us could see the shadows of our campfire reflecting off those big boulders. I'm also sure they could hear us as well. It was the perfect Halloween night movie setting.

The night air was chilly and the sky was very dark. But somehow, we could still see the outline of a few clouds lighted by a sliver sized moon. The wind had picked up slightly and we could hear it rustle through the trees. The light from our fire was flickering. We could hear the muffled voices of the Scouts below us, echoing up the cliff.

If you think something dramatic is about to happen, you are correct. But it is not what you think.

The stress of the previous two days was all but a memory when Ed let us in on his little secret. We were going to give the Scouts a night they were going to remember forever. His plan seemed harmless enough. So we went along.

Ed and his father would frequently hunt together and would spend a great deal of their time where we were camping. Ed's dad had even built a small cabin there. His dad would often leave his hunting arsenal in the cabin. This is 1968, remember, so leaving things like that around was not a big deal. Ed went into the cabin and came out a couple of minutes later with his dad's 12 gauge shotgun and a shell, which he promptly loaded in the shotgun.

Ed started complaining about the food. He yelled out loud enough to be heard by those below. "Bill, can't you do anything right?"

Bill yelled back, "You're an idiot! You don't know what you're talking about!"

The Scouts below had to hear this. "Why don't you get on your horse and get out of here?" Ed yelled even louder. For emphasis, he threw his arm up and pointed toward the horses.

Ed was rather animated. I doubt if the Scouts down below could see this. I guess it helped him get in character. He was a good actor. Even I thought he was serious.

Bill shouted right back. "I'm not leaving! You make me!"

The two of them were very close to the edge of the cliff. They wanted to make sure they were seen.

Ed fired the shotgun and they both fell away from the edge of the cliff and toward us. The shell exploding out of the barrel of that big shotgun lit up the night sky. The boom, I'm sure, could be heard for miles.

The four of us all got behind those big boulders and rolled them off the edge of the cliff. We could hear the occasional thud as they hit the side of the cliff on their way down. A few seconds later we heard them splash into the lake below.

As expected the entire troop gathered up their lanterns and headed for where they heard the splash. I think they stayed up all night looking for bodies.

When we awoke the next morning, we discovered our practical joke didn't go exactly as planned.

There were all kinds of people dragging the lake for bodies. They even had the county's volunteer scuba diving team searching.

After the incident with the bank robber, we were not about to let them in on our secret. I don't think Ed, Bill, or Jackson ever told anyone of the rolling stones. But now you know.

People talked about that bank robber, and the lake dragging for a long time. I just smile.

Little Pink Hearts in the Heat of the Night

I am just a common ordinary guy who lives in a small Southern Illinois town.

I have always enjoyed the slow pace a small town provides. Sometimes, though, things happen there that make it feel like a big city. For example, something happened in my hometown that we still talk about and celebrate today, forty years after the event took place. I'm nearly six decades old now, so the details may be a bit jaded, but this is my memory of it.

In the late sixties we were the location for a major Hollywood motion picture. Maybe you heard of it? "In the Heat of the Night." Big name movie stars were living amongst us for a few weeks. I'm talking Sidney Poitier, Rod Steiger, and Warren Oates. How much more big city can you get than that?

At that time we had a population of about 3,500 people and a good portion of them followed the film crew around. It, obviously, was a pretty exciting time for my little town. A few of our citizens were actually recruited for stand-in parts. One or two even spoke a line or two.

Rod Steiger's house in the movie belonged to a friend of mine.

When I would tell this story to my friends, I would tell them that Peter Bogdonovich was the Director of the movie. I just recently discovered I was wrong about that. Normon Jewison was the Director. That would not have made any difference to me anyway back then. As a high school kid, I was more impressed with the Hollywood stars. I didn't really care about the people behind the camera.

Anyway, the movie's director, Normon Jewison, stayed in the home of the Andersons who were friends of my Mom and Dad. The Anderson's home was one of the nicest houses in town. They were going to be gone on an extended vacation during the filming of the movie, so they agreed to let the director stay in their beautiful home.

I don't know if this really happened but I remember my parents telling me a story about the director's stay in the Anderson house. According to my parents, the house had a gas fireplace in it and they were very proud of it. In the sixties, I do not believe there were many gas type fireplaces in Southern Illinois. So, I guess that's why the Anderson's seemed to exhibit such feelings about their fireplace. Mom and Dad said they didn't use it much. They didn't want to mess it up. They used it only for atmosphere and esthetics.

Apparently, Normon did not understand, or did not care, about its purpose in life. Normon invited some of his friends over and cooked several meals in it. He never cleaned up his mess, apologized, or even offered to pay for his damages. To us "little people" that represented the attitude of the uncaring big city.

"In the Heat of the Night" had a racially charged theme. The setting for the movie was in Mississippi. But in the late sixty's there was so much tension in the South, that the movie producers were concerned about making that type of movie there. After checking out many other possible locations, they decided to film it in our Southern Illinois town.

For us, watching them make the movie was like watching a movie every day, all day long, for weeks on end.

I actually had the opportunity to watch a scene being filmed without the worry of being squashed by the crowd of movie watchers. I had the best seat in the house, so to speak.

The opening scene in the movie was about the town's deputy, Warren Oates, finding the dead body of the town's wealthy plant owner. That scene was filmed in the alley between my home and the abandoned building next door. My bedroom was located on the third floor. We had recently converted part of the attic into my bedroom. I could walk out of the lone window of my bedroom onto the flat roof over the second story. That roof was the perfect vantage point for observing what was going on in the alley beneath me.

I could watch from above without interfering. I literally had a bird's eye view. Because I was only about thirty feet above the filming, I wondered if I would hear the director yell "cut" as he pointed his finger at me, and then ask me to give up my perch. I guess I was OK because I was never asked to leave. Every time I watch that scene, I still look extra hard to see if my head is in that scene.

The crew arrived around six in the evening and didn't leave until around six the next morning.

I remember Warren Oates leaning over a man pretending to be dead. Not sure, but that dead body may have been one of our town's finest citizens.

Sidney Poitier, who was not in the scene, was leaning against a nearby building. Sidney Poitier was one of my favorite actors. I regret not getting his autograph. I was just too shy to ask him.

Before this scene could be filmed, though, the alley had to be lit up. I watched a member of the lighting crew grab a long extension ladder and place it on the abandoned building.

Next, he grabbed a light, which was attached to a tripod, hoisted it onto his shoulder, and then headed for the ladder. Remember this is the sixties. Necessary lighting was not small. The equipment on his shoulder looked about five feet long, heavy, and bulky. The guy carrying it up the ladder was huge. He looked like a defensive linebacker for the Oakland Raiders. I remember the Oakland Raiders back then were full of big, beefy, ominous looking fellows.

That lighting technician must have made a big impression on me because forty years later I still can clearly see him in my mind. He was dressed in a white t-shirt, blue jeans and red high top tennis shoes. This was forty years ago. Colorful tennis shoes were not something one was accustomed to seeing in Southern Illinois. Obviously, he was one of those Hollywood people we all thought we knew so much about.

The technician was three quarters of the way up the ladder when I heard the crowd on the ground let out a rather raucous laugh. They were all clapping their hands and pointing. That guy had stopped his progress up the ladder.

One hand was on the rung above him. The other was on the tripod he was escorting to the rooftop. His two feet were firmly planted on a rung below him. His blue jeans were now on the same rung as his feet, which obviously made his upward progress rather difficult, if not impossible.

That indeed was a funny site. But I'm sure that alone is not what everyone was laughing at. This big, burly, football looking guy, was trapped on the ladder with the bulky tripod on his shoulder and his pants around his feet. Covering his mid-section, though, was a large pair of white boxer shorts adorned with little pink hearts. Little pink hearts... not exactly what one might expect to see on a guy like that.

Amid all the commotion below him, he kept his

cool. He somehow managed to pull his pants back up and finish his assent up the ladder. How could he do that and not fall off? That was impressive. The ease with which he pulled up his trousers, though, made me wonder if this was not a common occurrence for him. I remember thinking he must have enjoyed the crowd's reaction. Perhaps he thought of himself as comic relief for the film crew.

It took twelve hours to film that thirty second scene, but it provided me with a lifetime of memories.

Hollywood spent quite a bit of money to make that film. I know that some of the town's people actually in the movie were monetarily compensated. Others were compensated for their inconvenience. Some like the Andersons were not appropriately compensated. My family was among those compensated. My parents were paid fifty dollars. But it wasn't for the inconvenience of a bright light shining in our bedroom windows all night long. It was for the right to have our name "up in lights." If you look real close, in the beginning of the movie, you will see our name in big bold letters.

We tried to get the movie to premiere in our little Southern Illinois town. I guess the Hollywood big shots considered our movie theater too small for them. Even back then, at my young age, I considered that a pretty arrogant attitude. Especially, after they took over our little town. Oh well, at least, they gave us an experience we still celebrate forty some years later.

"In the Heat of the Night" won the Oscar for best picture, I think, and my favorite actor, Sidney Poitier, was nominated for best actor. Rod Steiger played the town's Chief of Police, and he did a great job. He sure seemed to enjoy his gum. If you saw the movie, you know what I mean. I was disappointed when he was not

nominated for an Oscar. When I was in college, I had a poster of Rod Steiger hanging on the wall of my dorm room. It was a giant poster of him with gum in mouth and dressed in his Sparta police chief uniform.

I read someplace that "In the Heat of the Night" is considered one of the top one hundred movies of all time. And my little town, Sparta, was part of it. In addition to that, I can add that my family has their name displayed in a very prominent position in the movie. How cool is that?

During Sparta's 175 year anniversary, nearly fifty years after the release of the movie, we were visited by Scott Wilson, one of the movies actors. He was the young man seen running across the bridge while trying to evade Sheriff Gillespie.

This movie launched his career. Since his appearance he has had more than fifty film credits. For those of you who are fans of the TV show "The Walking Dead," you know him as Dr. Hershel Greene.

Even small towns can be the start of something big and quite entertaining.

Fowl Owl on the Prowl

Much of the movie *"In The Heat of the Night"* was made in my home town when I was a teen. My home town was chosen because of racial tensions in the Deep South of the 1960s. Most likely, the producers felt it would be easier to make their socially challenging movie somewhere other than in Mississippi. The setting for the movie was the fictional town of Sparta, Mississippi.

There were many rumors circulating about things that happened during the making of that movie. If they were true, it certainly is understandable why we were selected for the movie's actual filming.

One of the rumors was that while shooting an earlier scene in Mississippi, Sidney Poitier strongly felt the racial tensions of the Deep South. It was said he slept with a loaded pistol under his pillow. The better part of wisdom prevailed. They needed to find a new less stressful location. No actors would have to sleep with loaded guns under their pillows in Southern Illinois.

Another advantage to shooting the film here was that the producers would not have to change the city limits sign. I don't honestly know if that one is true, but we heard it a lot.

"In the Heat of the Night" was definitely an emotionally charged movie. The producers took quite a chance in making this movie. The struggle for Civil Rights was still being actively waged in America in 1967 when this movie was made.

A particularly sensitive scene in the movie was when a black man returned a slap to the face of a white wealthy man. Supposedly, that was one of the first times in a major motion picture that a black man reacted to a provocation from a white man. Even though the Civil Rights Act of 1964 had been enacted, the United States as a whole, had some pretty strong feelings on the issue of race.

Critics still refer to the scene as one of the most memorable. I am sure that is one of the reasons for its Best Picture academy award.

Regardless, Hollywood coming to Southern Illinois, and Sparta, in particular, was a big, big deal.

Many things stand out about those weeks Hollywood spent in town. Of course, some of us had the opportunity to get up close and personal with the actors. Lives were interrupted and gossip dominated conversations.

Some of my friends actually had the opportunity to sit down and "chat" with a couple of the actors. Sidney Poitier and Rod Steiger, they say, were not very sociable. Warren Oates, on the other hand, appeared to enjoy talking with the locals.

For me, the best part was being able to watch, up close and personal, the "dead body" scene being filmed right next to my home. I had a "bird's eye view" of that process and also the opportunity to speak with a couple of the actors. My shyness, though, prevented me from following through with speaking to the actors.

Those of us who lived through it have their own special memories. I have a friend who says his favorite memory was sharing his house with Rod Steiger. He played the town's sheriff.

I remember watching a big burly lighting technician trying to climb a ladder with his pink hearted white boxers around his knees. That was an absolutely hilarious experience.

Naturally, my English teacher, Mr. Grant, took advantage of the movie being here. He had all his students write an essay on what we considered our most memorable scene and why.

The most predominately chosen scene was the one where Virgil Tibbs and Eric Endicott, a wealthy plantation owner and a racist, exchange face slaps. That would be expected. I would agree. The face slap certainly was a memorable moment.

My memorable scene was and still is, though, probably different than most. I don't remember everything I wrote in my six page essay. I do remember, though, that I thought Mr. Grant was asking too much of us.

I am not one who spends valuable time analyzing movies. I never have been. But high school English teachers think their students should. I wrote great deal of fluff into my attempt to justify my memorable scene.

"In the Heat of the Night" was a great movie, no doubt. In 1960, racial problems were a major concern and the movie certainly addressed it. I didn't think I really had to write an essay about cultural anxiety. Everyone in America felt it. At least that was how I felt as a teenager.

Regardless how we all felt, Mr. Grant still required an essay. I wanted to be different, so my essay dealt with what I call "The Diner Scene."

It begins with Sidney Poitier, the Philadelphia detective and Warren Oates, the town's deputy, in the police car and getting ready to recreate the deputy's routine nightly activity. Part of his route is ultimately a stop at a local diner.

The two take off and then the scene shifts. We next see a hand holding what appears to be a dinner knife trying to pry a lock. The camera pans up following the knife. We hear a click. Another hand reaches inside a box with square letters and turns on the light inside.

Then we see the pockmarked face attached to the hands. I remember the huge Adam's apple.

The box turns out to be a juke box. A happy almost child-like melody begins playing. It sounded more like a children's lullaby. At first I thought it was "Little Red Riding Hood" by Sam The Sham and the Pharaohs.

The face of a man is only a few inches away from the juke box. He is intently listening. His head begins to bob up and down in time with the music, as does the hand not holding the knife. He steps away and starts the goofy dancing. And he never let go of the knife.

We finally get a good look at the guy. He's wearing a dirty apron; so he is not a customer. He is a tall, lean, man with sinewy build and greasy dark hair. The character creeped me out.

The creepy guy hears a commotion in the parking lot and goes over to the window to check it out. By now it is evident no one else is in the building.

He sees a police car drive up.

The worker evidently realizes who's in the car and walks across the small room to the counter. He sits on the counter, throws his long lanky legs over it, takes a pie off the shelf and puts it under the counter.

Once that's accomplished he starts tapping on the counter with that same knife, but in a different hand, swivels his hips back and forth, places a dim-witted smirk on his face and waits for the two men to enter. All the while we hear "Fowl Owl on the Prowl" playing in the background.

The men in the police car are getting ready to get out of their car. But before doing so, the deputy tells the detective that he plans to drink a soda and eat a wedge of pie.

Just then Rod Steiger, the chief of police, drives

up and angrily gets out of his police car and approaches the other two. The chief questions the detective as to his purpose. Heated words are exchanged and then finally all three enter the diner.

It's funny. I know significant things happened in that diner, but what I remember most is that weirdo character and because of him how that place could actually have any business. I certainly would not take any of my dates to a place like that.

No kidding! I really thought that.

Actually this diner scene was originally shot using Sam The Sham and the Pharaohs' song, "Little Red Riding Hood." The artist wanted more money than the producers wanted to pay, so they turned to Quincy Jones to write a new one.

He wrote it on the spot with a beat and theme to match the existing footage and intent. Like the planned original, Quincy Jones' song was an ode to a big bad predator.

The words of his song go:

"All you little birds better lock up tight 'cause there's a foul owl on the prowl tonight.
Hey, little lark, get outta the dark, Fowl owl on the prowl.
Cute little jay, stay outta his way, Fowl owl on the prowl.
You might be the quail he'll tail, Fowl owl on the prowl..."

It just seemed like a funny song to play in such a serious movie. I was not expecting funny.

At this point in the movie, one of the town's wealthy businessmen had been murdered and a couple of people already accused of committing it. One of the accused is the town deputy, which is why the big city detective and the deputy are in the car at the diner.

The song "Fowl Owl on the Prowl" appeared innocent. That unexpected innocence in the middle of a tense movie and the visual of a dancing small-town weirdo strongly suggested ominous things were going to follow. Even I could see that.

Ominous things did follow. The lanky weirdo guy showed up again a few more times in the movie.

The dancing guy reminded me of someone I thought was an actual resident of my fair city. We all knew some of the movie's extras were residents. I could not understand why he was given a speaking part.

I really had seen that guy before. His name is Anthony James. I had seen him as a minor character in several TV shows in the early 60′s.

Strange as it may be, that is the scene that impacted me the most. Perhaps that happened because Mr. James did such a good job of reminding me of someone I knew or thought I knew.

I worked hard on my essay and was expecting an "A" for my effort. I didn't get it. Mr. Grant gave me a "B+" He left a note saying he appreciated my uncommon approach to the topic.

The mayor and town council tried very hard to get the movie to premiere in Sparta, Illinois. They were unsuccessful. No one was surprised about that. Most expressed the belief that all actors were snobs anyway.

I personally wondered how we would be able to accommodate all those actors, their friends and families and all of our community in our little theatre. It was a physical impossibility. Most likely, the building could only seat one hundred or so. The town had a population of three thousand and you know every one of them would want to come.

Regardless, the town of Sparta, Illinois survived its Hollywood experience.

City Lake

In the fall of 1967, I met a beautiful red head. With God's guidance, our mutual friends, Dave and Cindy arranged for us to meet at a Friday night Lions Club dance. We were immediately attracted to each other.

I was shy and so was CJ. Perhaps that's why we were brought together. It was that shyness that kept us together and still does.

Dave and Cindy's relationship was not to be. Cindy found someone else, several times. Dave found Martha.

CJ and I would meet our friends almost every Friday night at the Lions Club Dance. I looked forward to showing off my red head and being with my friends.

I remember one particular Friday night dance in early May 1968.

CJ and I were to meet two other couples at the Lions Club. Dave was with Martha and Bobby was with Susan. It was a blast whenever we got together. Bobby was the only good dancer of the guys. All three of the girls were terrific dancers, though. Dan and I were always up to trying to not trip ourselves or our dates while on the dance floor.

The band was playing all the good songs; fast, slow, and in between. They were playing "96 Tears" when we entered. It was one of my personal favorites.

We strolled, twisted, watusied. We even did the swim. It seemed as if every song had its own dance. Dan and I attempted those and other choreographed dances. I tried to move my arms, shoulders, legs, and feet in a vain attempt to stay in time to the beat of the music. I honestly didn't care, though, how I looked. I was dancing with my baby.

The band played the great slow songs of the day: "And I Love Her" by the Beatles, "Surfer Girl" by the

Beach Boys, "When a Man Loves a Woman" by Percy Sledge.

I believed back then that those songs required me to dance as close as possible to my partner. I still believe that way. CJ and I certainly enjoyed feeling each other's hearts as we danced to those songs.

At ten thirty, CJ and I said our goodbyes and left the dance. City Lake was calling.

I had been there many times. But until I met CJ, its only purpose was to fish or camp with my friends.

The lane to the city lake was a tree lined half mile rocky road which opened up to a parking lot in front of the lake. The lake was surrounded on all sides by a heavy line of trees, except where the parking lot and a shoreline area had been cut out.

It was a manmade lake used by the city for its water supply. A pumping station was set back a few yards from the shore line. There were several picnic tables scattered about. During the day time, the site had lots of use but the place was off limits at night.

There was an indentation in the thick woods at the rear end of the parking lot. That indentation wasn't paved or rocked. It had been cut out by someone. The ground was grassy and hard. It appeared to go back into the woods, a hundred feet or so and was perhaps twenty feet wide. The land surrounding the lake was used by a local farmer and I think he sometimes used this spot to store some equipment.

After dating CJ for a while, I began to look at the indentation with a different perspective. The spot, I speculated, would be a great place to share with my red head when the time was right. I hoped it would be at night and that none of my friends shared the same thoughts.

I was both excited and anxious about sharing City Lake that night with my date. CJ really did not know why we were leaving the dance earlier than normal. I had not yet shared my lake plans with her.

Under threat of death, my brother had loaned me his 1955 red and white BelAir Chevy convertible. I reminded CJ we had a convertible and it would be a shame to not take advantage of riding around town with the top down. Most likely that opportunity would not come again. Fortunately, she agreed.

We took a couple of laps around town, top down. It was early May and the night air was chilly. That didn't really matter. We just turned on the heater. She was sitting next to me and my arm was around her shoulder. We were quite warm.

Then unbeknownst to the beautiful red head, I headed to City Lake. I had finally worked up the nerve to share that spot with her. I was sure that CJ did not object because she snuggled up even closer to me.

That half mile drive down the tree lined lane with my heart beating more rapidly than I could previously remember seemed to take forever. When we finally got to the parking lot, it was empty.

I was sure we were alone so I turned off the headlights and found my way to the cut and backed into it until I could sense a tree behind me. It was essential that I was far enough into the cut that our car could not be seen if someone ventured onto the parking lot. I turned off the engine and sat still for a moment. My heart was pounding and it felt like CJ's was too.

Except for the crickets, the night was quiet and cool.

We could see the lake and the stars above it, as we looked down the path we just backed in to. The cool of the night crept into the topless Chevy. I knew it wouldn't be long before we would feel its effect on us. The top had to go up.

I had never done what my brain was telling me I was about to do. And I felt my date could say the same.

Probably because I had never had such an experience before, I remember thinking I really had no interest in letting the birds in the tree branches above us in on what I hoped was about to happen. That was another reason for the top to go up. Self conscious, I guess.

The top was locked down and we could feel the temperature rise as the coolness escaped through the open windows only to creep back in a few seconds later. Temperature control would be important this night. Not too cold. Not too warm. So we rolled the windows about three quarters of the way up.

We sat there sat quietly for a few moments and watched the stars twinkle in the water. It was just like they wrote about in those famous love stories and movies. You know those beach blanket movies!

It made us feel like Frankie and Annette on the beach at night. I felt like breaking out in song. But, I knew, that would only ruin the mood.

Instead I made note of the starry sky and how they twinkled and shone so bright. My right arm was around her shoulders and her head was cuddled next to mine. I turned to my lovely red head, looked into her eyes, and said "I can't stop this feeling, deep inside of me. You've hooked me, Babe! I have a feeling we are forever." My plan was to seal that with a passionate kiss, but I didn't get to. Something unforeseen happened.

Our privacy was rudely interrupted.

Just as I was about to validate my feelings for her,

car lights appeared through the trees to our right. And they seemed headed for the parking lot.

A definite mood killer!

Our hope, of course, was that they would turn around and head back the way they came.

That didn't happen.

The head lights, now on the parking lot, disappeared from our view, yet we could hear noise from the engine and the rattle of tires on the asphalt pavement coming closer to us.

We watched as two red lights matched up with entrance to our supposedly hidden lane. The red lights continued in our direction until the car they were attached to finally parked next to us.

We gave some thoughts to ducking down below the windows but realized it would do no good. We were caught and also quite relieved it was not in an uncompromising position.

There was a couple in the car, of course. The couple in the car rolled the window down closest to us and they both said "What cha' doin?" It turned out to be Bobby and Susan. Apparently they were about to share our perfect location with each other.

Obviously, the mood was ruined.

They told us they didn't anticipate finding anyone there. They, like us, were expecting to share quiet time together. They apologized and left.

We were alone again. But our secret was out.

There was nothing else to do. I started the car, turned on the lights and got my date home just a little earlier than planned.

Our privacy had been violated and we were sure it would be again if we returned. It was the perfect location, we thought. The atmosphere, the quiet, the esthetics, the seclusion, the heart pounding emotion. It was all there. My red head and I knew we would never be able to match that exact combination again.

The Legend of Mad Myrtle

In a time, long, long ago, when I was young, there was a legend in a very specific geographical area of Southern Illinois. No one could escape it. It was real. It was a frightening legend. Yet many teens faced it. And I was no exception.

No one knew for sure how it began. There were many speculations and many attempts to verify whether it was fact or fiction. To this day, I am not satisfied as to which it is?

I don't hear much about the legend today. Perhaps the legend has ceased to exist? But if you talk with anyone who lived in Southern Illinois back then, they will tell you they remember!

This is my account of the legend of Mad Myrtle.

My girlfriend and I lived in different small towns and attended different high schools. We generally saw each other on Friday nights. But that didn't mean we didn't visit. We talked each and every night on the telephone. Like most teenagers back then, our parents complained to us about not being able to have ready access to the phone in the rare event they actually needed it.

We always shared with each other the important things about life. Things like: our school's sports teams, music, what our friends were doing, the good things and the bad things about our schools, whatever the current fad was, the Saturday night plans. etc. You know, the really important things to a teenager.

On date night, usually, we would eat somewhere and then take in a movie. The movie house was only open on week-ends, Thursday through Sunday. It showed one movie each night which ended about 9:00 p.m.

Frequently, after leaving the movie, we wound up

at the Lyons club. They always had a good local band playing. We would visit and dance with our friends until 11:30 p.m., when the band quit playing.

Back then, it seemed to be standard practice that all dates would end by midnight. Having the Friday night dance end when it did insured a satisfactory amount of time to get the dates to the appropriate house before the midnight hour.

Although my girlfriend and I lived in different towns, this practice still gave me time to get her home before midnight and amply wish her a goodnight. Her father had made it quite clear that I was to have her home by midnight. I understood the consequence if she was late getting home.

On one of our telephone visits, we both talked about the same strange thing. The talk that week in both schools apparently was about encounters several kids had the week-end before with a mysterious woman.

There had only been occasional conversation about her before. But everybody was talking about her now. The experiences were basically the same. No one could accurately describe the woman's appearance. Most thought she was an apparition. No one knew for sure where she came from or why, but they knew exactly where she lived.

There were plenty of speculations as to why she was there and what she planned to do while in the area. There were also plenty of rumors about what she would do to those she considered intruders into her domain. It was, to us, like we were living in our own horror movie.

What really made this story strange was that even though my girlfriend and I went to different schools the reports of the encounters were almost exactly alike. That certainly added validity to what we heard about the woman. We all knew her as Mad Myrtle.

As I said, it was unclear why she was here. There were many variations of her story. But, everyone agreed that if she felt you were an intruder you would come to know her personally. That of course meant your demise.

The funny thing is, though, that we all were 100% convinced that people disappeared because of her, yet no one could say who those people were. But that little fact didn't seem matter to us. It only mattered that people ceased to exist in our world, because of her.

There was one story most people gave for the reason for Mad Myrtle's existence in Southern Illinois. They say Myrtle was travelling through the area twenty years earlier with her family.

The car she was in ran out of gas. It was a very warm July day. For some reason, the local teenagers believed it to be in the beginning of July and for those of us who chose to explore this legend, the 4th of July celebration took on an additional meaning.

Before arriving here, Myrtle had recently married for the second time. Her first husband was killed in a horrible factory accident in an Ohio steel mill. She was in her early thirties and quite attractive and had three children ranging in age from fourteen to three. The death of her husband left her a very wealthy woman.

The man she just married, the legend says, was about eighteen or nineteen. It was a whirlwind romance.

Anyway, most likely it was a few hours before nightfall when her husband decided to leave the car and walk to the nearest town to get gas. Myrtle and her husband had been arguing, terribly. He had, in fact, threatened to kill her and the family. The story has no clear reason that I can remember, but things had cooled down, supposedly, when he left the car to get the gas.

He left her with instructions to stay in the car.

She never saw him again. Myrtle and her three children were left alone.

The reason for the argument was that Myrtle had apparently caught her husband in her bed with another woman. Myrtle had taken the children to a nearby community to see the circus. She loved her husband with all she had and never questioned him. And he apparently had never given her a cause to think otherwise.

The story was never clear as to why the husband was unfaithful. I guess it didn't really matter. The fact that he was unfaithful and Myrtle was wealthy helped to create a reason for her later actions.

Perhaps in an attempt to fix their problem, the entire family ended up in their car headed for some town in Southern Illinois. No one speculated on the reason for Southern Illinois. It didn't matter. It only mattered to our Mad Myrtle legend that they ran out of gas in that specific area. Some speculate that running out of gas was the husband's original plan and that he had once known a young lady in Southern Illinois.

According to the story, Myrtle decided to look for her wandering husband after a couple of hours. She gave her oldest son the responsibility to watch over the other two.

It was almost full dark when she finally returned to the car. She had not found her husband. But what she saw upon her arrival at the car surely turned her mad.

Her three children were a bloody mess. The two youngest were most certainly dead. Her oldest was barely breathing.

His last words to her were "It was a man and a woman! They were young." She vowed to avenge the death of her children and nothing or no one would stop her.

The assumption is that she died there trying to search out the killers. Her ghost returns every July because it is July when she lost her family.

The legend says she only seeks out young people.

That perhaps explains why so many young people took an interest in her.

As adults, most of us would dismiss this as pure bunk. Too many discrepancies and too much missing information. Teens do not really care about that. There was just enough information to have fun verifying.

My girlfriend and I decided that we would seek out the legend along with our friends, David and Carla.

Supposedly, there was a five to ten mile radius South and West of Sparta in which the ghost of Mad Myrtle could be found. Our plan, that night, was to eat someplace, show up for a short time at the dance, and then go out to our pre-selected spot.

If the truth be known, David and Carla were much more into the exploration of the Mad Myrtle legend than we were.

David had a convertible. It was hot. My date and I would enjoy being seen riding in the back seat with the top down. That alone was quite an invitation.

I could not tell you what we ate or what band was playing that night at the Lyons. But what happened after night fell is still stamped clearly in my mind decades later.

Let's not kid anybody here, we were teenagers and we planned to park the car in a rural area after dark. What we told each other, of course, was we were on a mission to find Myrtle.

In reality the mission was not necessarily to find a ghost. It only provided a legitimate excuse to park in the woods at night with the opposite sex. Perhaps teenage hormones would allow us to find success in other explorations?

All four of us found success that night. But it wasn't the success we really wanted.

We got to our destination about nine o'clock and talked for about half an hour. We needed to plan what to do when Mad Myrtle showed up. And then we got quiet. We wanted to make sure we could hear her coming.

By now darkness had completely engulfed us. It was a moonless starless night with just the slightest whisper of a warm July breeze.

We had been quiet for what seemed to be a very long time. Just listening! We were sure we had given Myrtle enough time to appear.

Our dates were sitting close. CJ's head was on my shoulder and my arm was around her keeping her close. I was the mighty Spartan, after all. My job was to protect her.

But it seemed this night Myrtle was not coming for us. So I decided it was time to explore other things. I sensed CJ felt the same.

Just as the hormonal explorations were about to begin, the back of the car seemed to dip slightly. We all felt it. What was it? Could it be?

Although we all looked around, nothing but darkness existed.

Then there was that horrible smell. Faint at first. Then it seemed to encompass us. It smelled like a dead animal. Yet, there was no evidence of that either. We had passed no dead animals.

I knew it was only seconds, but it seemed like moments.

If it was Mad Myrtle, we were in serious trouble.

Had she come for us after all? We needed to leave immediately, if not sooner.

Why was David not starting the car? Suddenly, from the back of car, there was a blood curdling scream. And then we felt the back of the car violently move up and down.

She was indeed coming for us. She would reach CJ and me, first.

I had only a blink of an eye to react. But what would I do?

I heard a scream! It was Carla. I did not think Carla could scream any louder.

My girlfriend was screaming too. I knew she was, but no noise was coming from her mouth. My heart felt like it was going to pound right out of my chest.

And David? He was tearing up. His mouth was closed. I could hear no noise from him but his shoulders appeared to slightly twitch up and down.

Then it seemed as if the trunk of the car was going to dislodge itself from the rest of the vehicle. I looked backward and thought I saw something.

The hair on my arms stood up.

We all screamed at David to start the car up and get out.

But it sounded like David was laughing. It sounded like true laughter, not some heinous laughter from someone taken over by an apparition.

The back of the car bounced up and down again. Several figures jumped out from behind it. All were laughing uncontrollably. And now, so were David and Carla.

Everything suddenly became abundantly clear. My girlfriend and I had been set up.

David and I were close friends, but I had forgotten

that he enjoys creating drama. He created this one with Carla and some friends.

Before we left the area, my friend was kind enough to explain how he and his friends accomplished his scheme.

I must say I was not happy to be the recipient of his prank. It took me some time to live it down.

David became a legend in his own right at our school. Eventually, I was proud to know I had helped him obtain that status.

As far as the Mad Myrtle legend is concerned? It really did exist. If she was there that night, I hope she had a good laugh as well.

I was a senior in high school when I had my personal Myrtle experience. That was probably the last noteworthy adventure I had before leaving the comforting confines of my home town.

Life had called me away.

As Captain Kirk would say at the conclusion of every successful mission when his navigator would ask him what coordinates to set the starship to, he would only say "Out There!" and wave his hand in a forward motion.

So off I went to explore my uncharted worlds. College was waiting and so were three separate career ventures and a family. It would be twenty five years before this mighty Spartan could return home.

I think I've grown up a little since then.

Grandpa Bill

I loved my Grandpa Bill. Everybody did. He was quite a character and a great storyteller. His stories were fascinating. Most believed them to be fiction, but he told them as if they were true.

He told them with such conviction, I, for one, believed they were true? Perhaps they were a bit embellished, but I always assumed them to be based on fact.

To me, he was relating history and he made history exciting. Mostly, he talked about the old West. He lived during the same time as some of the most famous Western characters.

Grandpa Bill was my dad's stepfather. I never knew my Dad's real father. He died just after my Dad was born. Grandma married Grandpa Bill a few years later.

Bill was a very friendly guy and liked by everyone he met. Grandpa frequently alluded to friendship with old-west cowboys, both hero and villain. Several well-known cowboys were still alive in 1920 when he took up residence here. So knowing some of them certainly added to Grandpa's mystique. When Grandpa moved to Southern Illinois he bought some land, and started raising the horses he brought with him.

His arrival was quite an event. You see, he actually drove his herd of horses from Southwest Missouri to his new ranch in Illinois.

According to the newspaper accounts of his day, Grandpa's drive was backed up by some of those old famous gunfighters.

Two of them were Wyatt Erp and Bat Masterson. Grandpa Bill had apparently struck up a friendship with them at some point in his past. In 1920 Erp and Masterson were too old to actually be part of a trail drive but they were intrigued by Grandpa's modern day trail drive to Illinois and invested in his undertaking.

It was nothing for Grandpa to be seen walking around his ranch with a pearl handled pistol inside his ornate holster strapped to his hip. There were still snakes on his ranch to be dealt with; he would tell us.

When I turned ten, he said I was old enough to learn about guns. With Mom and Dad's approval, we then spent many hours behind the barn at his personal range.

He was eighty when we started and still very capable. Many hours were spent learning gun safety before he taught me how to draw and fire. Nothing fancy, just how to be accurate.

"It's not the speed of the draw," he insisted, "but the accuracy that really matters."

I believed him. He never missed what he was aiming at.

One of Grandpa's special delights was sitting around a campfire at night telling his stories. Those campfires were an event, actually. He would invite his wranglers, neighbors, and friends. Someone would always bring the beef or pork for him to cook in the pit built especially for these events.

Whenever I attended these campfire events, and it was often, I would help him prepare. My reward was sitting with his friends and listening to their adventures. Even as a very young child, I always looked forward to hearing them.

His two wranglers reminded me of my perception of real life cowboys.

Like the real cowboys of the old West, their only possession was a saddle. Grandpa still had a hundred horses and these men enjoyed the hard work required to keep them healthy.

I don't think they were old. But as a youngster, I thought they were. They looked haggard and worn. Their skin was tanned and leathered. Their hands were calloused.

I am sure they could have had other employment, but they had worked for Grandpa for as long as I could remember. More evidence of the kind of man my Grandpa was.

We had a special bond, he and I. I did not completely understand why, but I knew we were connected somehow. I always wondered why we felt so connected. He frequently hinted at it, but would never completely substantiate anything.

On 9 October 1970 we were celebrating his birthday and mine. And, of course, it involved campfire stories. It was his 100th. and my 20th. Grandpa still reveled in his story telling. What a very special day it was.

Shortly after his centennial birthday party I became even more connected to Grandpa Bill.

My Grandpa was outlaw Bill Longley's son. This man was often the subject of his stories. Many thought they were just stories but on his 100th birthday Grandpa produced evidence.

You may be thinking, "Who is Bill Longley?"

Bill Longley was an actual person. Not some fictitious Western outlaw created by Hollywood. And grandpa was right about Longley being an historical person. I have a book written by George Turner, a noted Western historian. William P. Longley is one of the outlaws he researched.

According to Mr. Turner, Bill Longley was a nasty man, even by outlaw standards. As evidence of that statement, Mr. Turner wrote that once, "Bill had turned to bounty hunting and after getting his man, he used some of the reward money to buy a new pair of guns." Just to see if those guns worked properly, Turner said, "Longley tested them out on a passer- by. The local sheriff came to arrest Bill and was shot dead for his effort."

Like most outlaws, Longley spent much of his life running from the law. Finally, one day in late June 1877, the outlaw Bill Longley, was captured, convicted of murder, and hung two years later. He had literally been unsuccessfully hung twice before and somehow escaped death both times.

It was at his third and final hanging, Longley supposedly was heard saying that he was deserving of hanging and that it was his favorite way to die other than by natural death.

He was twenty seven when the rope finally snapped his neck, until he was "dead, dead, dead."

So is the story of outlaw Bill Longley as told by George Turner and often confirmed by my Grandpa, Bill Longley Jr.

Grandpa loved telling these and other details about the man he called his dad. As far as I knew, those types of details, he could have gotten from the same book I picked up in Tombstone, Arizona when I was a vacationing there with my mom and dad a few years before.

But I was most intrigued when he spoke of the kinder and gentler Bill Longley. Grandpa always spoke as if he had personal experience of that side of Bill senior. History very seldom portrays the outlaw in this manner.

My Grandpa produced evidence that he was

indeed the son of an outlaw.

William P. Longley Jr., my Grand dad was still very active as he entered his tenth decade of life, yet he was very much aware that his time was nearing its end. He also knew how much I enjoyed learning history of the old west. Perhaps that was our connection?

I spent many hours listening to him tell me about his first hand knowledge of the 'ol West. It wasn't the same as the history taught in school. This was real stuff.

When Grandpa spoke, I easily could visualize Bill Longley doing one of his dirty deeds. It seemed like I was standing next to his outlaw father.

I guess because I expressed such an interest, that is why he chose to give me his prized possession. Even that was presented to me in what I considered an old western style.

He had me follow him to his barn and told me we were about to have some fun. I had just bought my own authentic six shooter and I expected we were going to fire it for the first time.

The fun I expected was not what Grandpa had in mind. Grandpa told me I was going to help him remove the loot he buried a long time ago.

Could it be stolen money from one of Bill Longley's bank jobs? And why would my Grandpa still have it?

I followed my Grandpa to the back the barn where instructed me to remove a pile of hay. Under it he told me I would find a trap door. Beneath the door would be a locked strong box.

"I have the key." he said.

"I want you to use it to open the box."

Grandpa then handed me his six shooter which he removed from his old personalized gun belt. I had not seen Grandpa wear that belt for a coupl of years. But on this day his "special shooter" was prominently displayed in that belt for all to see. I do not know how he acquired his "special pistol" and that belt but he took pride in it and maintained it well.

The rumor was that he used it when he once helped Wyatt Erp catch an outlaw. I had my doubts about that one. He never denied it nor did anyone try to challenge its validity. It was too much fun to believe, I guess.

Even at Grandpa's advanced age, he still stood tall with that gun strapped to his hip. I did not believe it to be loaded anymore. It was just for appearance.

"Aim it, like I taught you, at the lock on the box. I want you to have what's inside."

I was surprised when the gun fired. The lock broke open as a result of the bullet from the gun hitting what it was aimed at.

Grandpa must have told the others at the party what we were doing because no one came to check out the noise I just made.

I took the box out of the hole and opened the lid to find something wrapped in an old linen cloth. Inside the linen cloth was a notebook. It was Bill Longley Jr.'s diary.

Why it was buried in hole in the back of the barn, I will never know. Grandpa Bill never had a chance to tell me. At the time I lifted the linen cloth out of its old resting place, he was more interested in explaining its content than in why he buried it.

The diary was about the life of his infamous outlaw father and his illegitimate son, my grandpa.

Even George Turner did not have access to this information. But I now do. He made me promise that I keep his diary a secret until after he's gone. I was surprised by his request, but gladly agreed. He was my Grandpa, after all. And I loved and respected that man.

Grandpa died the next day. He was 100 years and 1 day old.

There was, of course, a grieving period. His death was hard for me. Even at age 100, I believed he could still ride and rope. He always did tell everyone his goal was to reach 100 and not a day longer. I chose, though, not to believe him. To me, he was immortal.

He still had that twinkle in his eye and a gitty-up in his walk up to and including that day he gave me the diary.

About a month after grandpa left us, I decided it was time to explore his diary. If it was half as exciting as the man who wrote it, I was going to have a difficult time putting it down. That diary lived up to expectations and more.

Grandpa Bill always loved telling stories about the old west. The diary was full of them and I believed every word I read. In 1970, it was not myths I was reading; it was a retelling of history.

He was a devout Christian. Even those cowboy stories reflected Christian morals.

I am not so sure, though, everything in the diary wasn't somewhat stretching of the truth a bit. Most likely Grandpa was emulating Parables he found in the Bible.

He lived a very long time. He had many friends and was a positive influence on their lives, especially mine. Even today, when I least expect it, the life of Grandpa Bill and his teachings influence me.

Little Warriors

CJ and I have been married for over forty years. That's a long time in today's world. We believe in the pledge we made to each other. That pledge was "Until death do us part." If it is worth having forever, it's worth fighting for. Through those years there have been good times and some not so good times. There will be more of each, I'm sure. My warrior princess and I will fight through those as well.

From the moment we decided we could not live without each other, we knew having and raising children were going to be part of our life. But our children did not have the opportunity to be born in Sparta. Life had called the two of us away for a time.

One night in late 1974 my wife surprised me by telling me we were going to be blessed with our first child. At the time we were living at Ft. Leonard Wood, Missouri. We were excited. Our family plans were coming together.

I don't believe our pregnancy experience was any different than what most couples say they experience in a normal pregnancy. And ours was normal, except for the day of delivery. I had a horrifying adventure.

I believed I was prepared. I didn't miss a single Lamaze class. I would be a great assistant for my wife. I could handle the delivery of my expected baby boy. No problem!

Let me tell you this. Birthing classes DO NOT adequately prepare the man for what happened to me that day.

Sure, they have you visit the labor room, and explain what goes on there, and what the man and woman's individual responsibilities are. They even give you clues as to how to put your anxiety in check. But, let's be real here. The birthing process just does not happen exactly the way the professionals planned it to happen.

My wife was just beginning to have contractions as we got settled into the room. They hooked her up to the appropriate machinery. CJ didn't seem to be much concerned about her surroundings. I had learned to trust her, so I put whatever concerns I may have had aside.

CJ was relaxed. I was mentally going over my personal checklist: check the time between contractions, wipe her brow, comfort her, etc. I had the easy job. My wife had to do all the work.

I was confident "baby boy" was coming into this world without complication.

But then, from somewhere, I heard a woman scream and it was not my wife. Almost immediately, I heard what appeared to be the same voice yell, "You *moron!*"

CJ heard it to because she was as wide-eyed as I must have been. We were both trying to figure out what we just heard and how all that related to our environment.

"You *idiot!* Don't you ever touch me again!" the voice screamed.

All my training was useless now. No one had prepared me for this. It didn't help that my wife was now smiling. The screaming, my wife's smiling face, and the noise coming from the equipment attached to her belly was way too much information for my mind to process. To say I was about stressed out to the max would be an understatement.

Suddenly my wife started squeezing my hand. What was I supposed to do? Oh yeah! That was code for "contraction starting, check time, help her breath, and keep track."

My brain kicked back into reality time just as I heard another bloodcurdling scream. This time, though, I figured out the screaming was coming from the room across the hall. We were not the only expectant couple that night.

"You frigging moron. You're the reason I hurt like this. Don't you ever get near me again, or I'll make sure you can't do this to me again." I distinctly heard every single word that expectant mother said to the husband in the room with her.

"Did she no longer want her husband?" I thought. "Is my CJ going to feel the same?"

The similar reaction I was bracing for didn't come. Instead CJ started to laugh.

The lady across the room screamed again. I was scared out of my wits. What was going to happen in my room? I certainly couldn't ask my wife. She was smiling at me. I did not think that was normal under these circumstances.

Finally CJ shared her thoughts. "That lady across the hall from us is an RN and has a bi-week rotation in the OB ward. You'd think she'd have a better understanding of what's going on than the rest of us. She ought to know better than to be screaming like that. Her husband is a soldier stationed here. He has to take all that from someone who should know what to expect. Poor guy.

You looked kind of worried. You didn't really pay any attention to that stuff, did you?"

"What? Me? No, of course not, honey. Why would I?"

Our son, Pierre Jacque Russey II, was delivered into the world, without complication, a few hours later.

Petey was a blessing. After nine short months, he succumbed to a childhood disease. We still miss him.

God blessed us with another baby boy during the Christmas season of 1978 while I was stationed at Ft. Bliss, Texas. Richard Theron Russey was born in William Beaumont Army Medical Hospital in El Paso, Texas. Like his brother before him, Richard's arrival orchestrated an adventurous arrival. This time, for someone else.

CJ's parents decided to come to El Paso that year to spend Christmas with us and, if lucky, would be there for their Grandson's birth. They bought their tickets, boarded the plane, and safely arrived in sunny El Paso, Texas on Christmas Eve.

We were to meet them at the airport. CJ was already a little over one and a half weeks past her due date. To the untrained eye (and, of course, mine was trained), she looked as if she could deliver any moment. The expectant mother, though, was not having any problems and was excited to see her parents.

As her parents approached us, her dad's eyes were the only thing we could see. If they were any larger, they would have surely popped out of their sockets. My son's namesake, Richard, didn't even say hello. He looked at my wife's belly, grabbed her by the arm, and said, "We've got to go to the hospital now! Why are you here?"

My wife was amazing. She calmly assured her dad that she wasn't having any discomfort and she wasn't in imminent danger of delivering any time soon.

Neither I, nor CJ, nor CJ's mom showed signs of stress, so Richard felt better. We gathered up their bags, loaded them in the car, and headed for the nearest Kentucky Fried Chicken for lunch, obviously a sure sign that all was right in the world. KFC, you see, was my Father-in-Law's favorite place to eat.

My In-Law's Grandson was born three days after Christmas. They were able to stay for his birth. Even today, I can still see those huge eyes my Father-in-Law displayed at the El Paso International Airport.

A few years later our daughter, Brianna Paige, decided to show up in the middle of a snowstorm. We were living in Southern Illinois but many miles from my home town.

As anyone who lives in Southern Illinois knows, winters are unpredictable.

Winters can be bitter cold, warm, rain, or snowy. When our daughter was born, we were suffering through the worst snowstorm in decades. The State Police were strongly encouraging everyone to stay in their homes and not use the roads.

Snow had been falling heavily for two or three days with no sign of stopping. In the middle of this storm, our baby girl decided it was time to come out and play in the snow.

While CJ called her parents to tell them to meet us at the hospital, I blazed a path to our car. Then loaded up CJ and our son into the car and headed for the hospital. It was a drive which usually took about thirty minutes. On this day, though, road crews were struggling to keep the roads somewhat passable.

Driving on snowy roads is always stressful. The roads that day required an extraordinary amount of concentration. Many times I had to have faith that the road was actually under my tires. Fortunately, my three year old son seemed to understand what was happening. Thankfully, my warrior princess was still in charge of her labor. An hour after leaving our house, we pulled into the hospital's parking lot just behind CJ's parents.

We were thankful for that. They were in charge of

Richard. CJ and I were in charge of birthing the baby sister.

A few minutes later, we were both in the labor room. A few hours later, CJ was wheeled into the delivery room. I followed them in. The nurses, CJ, and I waited, and then waited some more for the doctor. Our daughter wanted out.

A few minutes later the doctor finally arrived still wearing his suit and tie. The attending nurse said the tie would be in the way. The doctor told the nurse to pin the tie to his back so it would be out of the way. The nurse carried out the order by grabbing a pair of scissors. She thought it would be faster than trying to find a pin, I guess.

The snow was still on the ground when we took Brianna home. Our family was now complete. We delivered our children into those distant lands.

But, always, our plan was to return home. Home to Sparta. We fought battles in faraway lands. It even looked for a while as if we would never return to our beloved home.

We soldiered on, until, finally, a path was found that brought us home to stay. Our young children would have the advantages of being raised in my home town. But, of course, that didn't mean our battles were over. With children, they never are. Ours were just going to be fought on familiar grounds.

Lawful Consequences

CJ and I worked hard to ensure our children were prepared to face life on their own. It was important that our children understood authority and accountability. Sometimes, though, despite parent's best effort, children find a way to experience life as they see fit.

We insured their needs were taken care of, but we felt the practice of giving them their every want would make life too easy for them. Life, as we all know, is not always easy and there are consequences to deal with. Here are a couple of examples.

After being away from my home town for nearly twenty years, I had finally managed to move back to Sparta. CJ and I had two young children. The oldest thirteen and the youngest ten. We had moved into a nice neighborhood which had other young children. Both our children were quick to make friends. Especially Brianne.

Our daughter, Brianne, had an encounter with the long arm of the Sparta Police Department. She was about ten years old at the time. Brianne was not really involved in illegal activities. She just thought she was.

One night, Brianne was engaged in a game of flashlight tag with the neighborhood kids. After about thirty minutes, our daughter along with two of her friends came running, panting, into the house. We, of course, reminded them that flashlight tag required darkness. Their flashlights wouldn't help them in the house and what they were looking for was outside.

But they were excited and even seemed worried about something. We thought perhaps something unpleasant was going on outside. After catching their collective breaths, they finally told us they were running from the cops, and they were right behind them.

CJ and I looked out the door and noticed our city's

protector was making his nightly rounds. We knew that to be a routine, but chose not to remind Bree and her friends. This situation required a bit more parental investigation.

After a bit of prying, the young ladies told us they had been shining their flashlights into a vacant house when they noticed the cop car coming. They rather excitedly exclaimed "the cops are after us."

My wife and I both thought the situation was a perfect opportunity for a life lesson. We did not tell them the police car was in the neighborhood as part of a regular routine. Instead we told them to never run from the police. If stopped by them and you think you are in the wrong, fess up to it.

They apologized to us for looking in the house and went back outside. A few minutes later Bree came back. Flashlight tag was over.

Despite our objections, our son, Rich, bought a motorcycle. CJ and I had spent many late nights explaining our objections. Three days or so after his eighteenth birthday, Rich told us he had purchased a motorcycle with his own money and there was nothing we could do about it because he was of legal age to do so.

We were disappointed and expressed our disapproval. But he bought it with his own money, and we knew he worked hard to earn the money to buy it. Of that fact we were proud. This choice, though, would come with a consequence.

Rich and his buddies went on many rides together. They were teenagers, so their rides weren't always what I would consider pleasure rides. These teenage riders were learning to pop wheelies and ride standing on their bike seats. They would practice their stunts on a little used Sparta back road and then talk about them at school.

If one is doing illegal activities, one should not brag about them at school in front of everyone. One should be selective as to where bragging is done.

Needless to say, Sparta's finest was alerted to a dangerous secret activity by a local "biker gang" and where and when it would take place. My son and several of his friends were known members of that gang.

I don't really believe this particular gang, though, quite fit the image I had of biker gangs. They didn't ride loudly through town wearing studded black leather jackets, disrupting other people's lives. Nor did any of them engage in dishonest activities. They were teenage boys riding "crotch rocket" motorcycles, not the big bulky motorcycles ridden by unsavory characters.

These teenage boys chose an area very seldom used by the public. Their intent was to safely develop and practice new riding skills without the worry of endangering others. What they were doing on that back street was illegal, though, and quite dangerous.

Apparently, parents of one of Rich's buddies were unaware of this activity until the boys decided to brag about it at school. In an attempt, I guess, to prevent their son from injuring himself, a call was made to the police. A cruiser was sent to the secret location and caught them in the act of "dangerous and unsafe riding."

The police officer knew all the boys in this awful "biker gang." He let them all off with only a stern warning. An advantage, no doubt, of living in a small town.

I am aware the activity continued after this incident, but not at that location. I know this because Rich, a few years later, shared a video someone had taken of their practice sessions. Unbeknownst to us, though, and probably even Rich, our son was using those skills to develop a new hobby: motorcycle road racing. But that is another story.

Arachnophobia

As the body gets older, it tends to break down. One cannot escape it. Every last one of us has to deal with it. But we all deal with it in different ways. I'm OK with getting older. But occasionally, I wonder if I am really equipped to handle it.

I'm over sixty now and often times my mood determines how I deal with getting older. Sometimes an experience can determine how I feel. Sometimes, and I hate to admit this, watching a movie can affect how I deal with age.

On Super Bowl Weekend 2011, I had an adventure with some local spiders. On that weekend, John, a fellow teacher, had invited me along with some other friends to a Super Bowl Party at his new cabin. He had finalized the purchase a couple of months before. With his wife's blessing, John along with our help was going to turn this into his man-cave.

He said his cabin was in an isolated wooded area several miles from town. His man-cave was completely surrounded by trees. Whoever built it had great taste, because it looked somewhat like the home the Cartwright's lived in.

The previous owners never got a chance to live in it or complete their plans. They nearly had it ready for livability. It had city water. The electricity was hooked up. The geothermal heating and cooling system was installed. Just flip the appropriate switches and move in.

John said the couple divorced and had to sell.

His man-cave, though, had sat vacant for at least two years. It needed some attention before the party. The day before the Super Bowl Party, John invited me to help him clean it up and prepare it for our friends. He didn't think there would be great deal to do. A little sweeping and gathering logs for the fireplace was all he said it needed. I was pretty sure John exaggerated a bit. But I was up for it, so I packed my gear and headed to my buddy's house.

It was mid-afternoon when we arrived at our weekend retreat. John's description of the cabin was accurate. It really did remind one of the Ponderosa, but on a smaller scale. John wanted to show me around the cabin before unpacking his truck. I was impressed.

As soon as we arrived at the front door, John opened it. The first thing I saw was not what I was expecting. Glistening in the sunlight, stretched from the top of the door jam to the ceiling was a cob web. A big Halloween looking one, with honeycombed threads suspended by a thick single line on each end which attached the web to the door and the ceiling. Let me be perfectly clear here! "I hate spiders!" Spider webs mean spiders have been or are present. I was certainly hoping the resident of this web was long gone. Although I did not see the spider, I worried about where it was.

Even though it was early February, the cabin was infested with them. I bet I encountered three or four of those arachnids all weekend. And a couple of them were even attached to their web with what looked like some of their food.

In spite of this first web sighting, I moved on. John showed me the rest of the cabin, then we unpacked his truck and began the clean up. Considering how long the place sat empty, it really wasn't that messed up. After about three hours of removing the dirt and cob webs, we were satisfied with our clean up. We could finally put the weekend's groceries away and the beer on ice. We ate some sandwiches and tackled our next chore, relaxing.

My idea of what's relaxing and John's idea are not

necessarily the same. For me, one of those beers would taste good. That's all I need. More than that would insure the unique sounds of the great outdoors would not be quite so peaceful. I would have been content with just listening.

But John had other ideas. He was anxious to try out his big screen sixty inch TV equipped with an expensive surround sound system. Apparently, he had arranged to have it hooked up earlier in the week when he had the satellite service turned on.

I must admit the TV looked awfully funny in that big family room. There was no other furniture in it except the TV trays, two folding chairs, and a slightly worn couch. The couch was a nice added touch.

Watching the Super Bowl on that large screen with a bunch of guys was going to be fun. John figured he and I could test it out for quality of enjoyment. He planned to watch a movie and preview some past football games. That way we could insure the "sounds" of football were perfect. Nothing but the best for his friends!

A previous Super Bowl game was selected and placed in the CD slot. When the game came on, John played with the knobs on the sound system until he was satisfied. He only brought one movie and it was now time to enjoy it.

John pretty much knows what he is doing all the time. And I am sure his movie selection was no exception. I was told the movie was a comedy. I enjoy a good comedy. This one was entitled "Arachnophobia." When I questioned my buddy about it having spiders in it and being a comedy, he said, "Don't worry, It has Jeff Daniels and John Goodman in it." They're comedians so it had to be funny.

Although I never said anything, I doubted it was a comedy. John was smiling throughout the entire credits.

A movie of any kind about spiders would never be my choice. But I was bound and determined not to give my buddy the satisfaction of watching me squirm. It was only a movie, after all and not reality.

I must say I was proud of myself. I don't believe I squirmed even once.

In my mind, there is nothing funny about a large deadly spider from the jungles of South America accidentally transported to a small California town. According to the movie, it mates with a local spider and produces thousands of offspring. The residents of that California town disappear as a result of spider bites.

Sure the spiders are exterminated and comedians Jeff Daniels and John Goodman do some funny things, but spiders in any setting make me extremely uncomfortable.

After the movie ended, John critiqued his favorite parts. He reminded me that spiders are carnivores and eat by sucking their prey's innards out before ingesting them. I swear, he took a bit too much pleasure in describing how, John Goodman, the exterminator, and Jeff Daniels, the good doctor, liquidated the spiders. Something's just not right with my buddy, John.

I endured his critiques a little longer, drank beer number three, and convinced John I was too tired to stay awake. I found my sleeping bag and spread it out on the floor in front of the fireplace.

John then spread his bag out on the couch and turned out the light. (It was John's place so he got the couch.) He was snoring a very few minutes later.

But not me. The cabin was quiet, which meant that the arachnid was looking for me. Remember, I saw that vacant spider web at the door's entrance a few hours earlier. Maybe it was looking for me? At least with the quiet, I could hear its approach. Boy! The mind can do terrible things when it becomes inactive!

Reluctantly, I feel asleep.

I awoke to the sounds of scratching. The sounds seemed to be coming from the couch. They were muffled, barely audible. Or at least, that's what my sleepy brain was telling my ears they were hearing. I was facing the fireplace, so I couldn't be sure of what I thought I was hearing. I had to find out, so I turned toward the sounds. My heart stopped instantly.

I couldn't help myself. I screamed like a banshee. What was left of John was being sucked up into that giant spider's mouth.

I somewhat regained my composure. I needed to think. Rescuing John was out of the question, now. To survive, I had to get out of there as quietly and quickly as possible. Hopefully, it wouldn't see me and come after me.

But, my hopes were dashed. It was headed straight for me, a foot dangling from that thing's mouth.

There was no way I could escape. No where to go!

I froze. I remember thinking, "This is really it. I'm going to die. What is death going to be like?"

A sticky leg from that freak spider was reaching for me. It would be just an instant now.

Suddenly my eyes popped open. It was pitch black, but yet I knew my eyes were open. My body was moving from side to side. I felt a hand pushing me from side to side. "Could it be John's? Are we in the spider's belly?"

Then I heard what sounded like a man's voice. It was barely audible. I couldn't make out what he said, at first. But it sounded like "Are you OK?"

The pushing continued.

Then very quickly, everything came together. I heard John, emphatically, but with great concern, say, "Pete, Are you OK? Wake up, Pete. You must be dreaming!"

Whew! It was only a dream. But I wasn't so sure I wanted to admit that to my buddy. The middle of the night was not the time to deal with the razzing the admission would bring on. And John enjoyed razzing.

What do you do in a moment like that? Do you lie and say "Nothing's wrong. You must be mistaken!" Do you tell the truth? "Yea man, I had a nightmare." Or maybe you explain it away with some kind of plausible deniability. "It was all that beer, man. It made me have a bad dream."

I chose plausible deniability.

John seemed to accept my explanation. He admitted the beer must have had an effect on him as well. I doubt, though, he had the same problems with his sleep. We talked a few more minutes and he went back to his couch. Snoring soon followed.

I made the attempt to do the same. But with one eye open. That spider might come back.

Purple Leathers and the Motorcycle Gang

I have a riding buddy. We take every opportunity we can to get out in the countryside and just relax. He has a black Harley Davidson Road King Classic Touring motorcycle decked out with lots of chrome, equipped with saddle bags, radio, the works. I have a Honda Silverwing motor scooter. I call her "Red."

John looks like a typical Harley rider. He's not a great big guy, probably hovers around 5'10". But he is solidly built, very muscular, and he enjoys his long shoulder length wavy graying hair. His wears a full face beard and mustache (both matching his hair color) with a great deal of pride. He is constantly stroking it as if he wants to make sure it gets noticed.

Often we ride the back roads of Southern Illinois. On those days I would usually ride over to John's house and we would leave from there. Watching John prepare for our ride was an adventure in itself. John would don his black leather jacket, black leather chaps, and mid calf black boots.

We ride with helmets. My buddy always took care to insure his helmet didn't cover up all the hair. One hand would hold the helmet. He would place his free hand on his forehead and then slide it toward the back of his head to flatten the hair. He would then grab his ponytail and ceremoniously place it on his left shoulder. Then he would grab the left side of the helmet with his now freed up hand. With both hands he would lift the helmet above his head, and carefully slide it over his mane, all the while insuring that his ponytail stayed put. I never did understand why the placement was so important. After all, as soon as forward movement began, he no longer had control of placement.

The helmet was special. John fought in the Vietnam War and he was proud of his service. The helmet reflected his feelings. A decal of his old unit as well as the American flag covered every square inch.

Honestly, I was proud to be seen with him. He let me in on some of the hardships he had endured while a POW there. But that is another story.

My buddy loved his leather motorcycle apparel. He said he bought the gear shortly after getting home from Vietnam. The motorcycle he bought then had long since worn out as did the next three.

"These leathers will never, ever wear out," he told me every time he would put them on. But after several decades of riding a problem was developing he did not want to see, let alone admit.

Since the purchase of these leathers, his frame had expanded, somewhat. It was an ordeal to fit his body in that outfit. I would joke that I could see some stitches pop out. He ignored the comment. Somehow, he managed to work himself into his treasured leathers. Once that was accomplished, off we'd go. To this day, I don't know how he could breathe. But John didn't complain about that.

His complaints were directed toward the growing number of wear marks and holes appearing in his jacket. You might say the jacket was unsightly. Some wear marks and holes on a leather jacket are OK. They add character. John's jacket, though, looked more like homeless than rugged. The homeless appearance was beginning to get to my riding buddy. I was sure that a new set of leathers was coming sooner or later. From the look of the jacket, it would most likely be sooner.

One day, our riding experience totally changed and I was not prepared for it. No one could have seen this one coming.

As usual, I arrived at John's house around 10:00

a.m. We were planning to ride to Garden of the Gods in The Shawnee National Forest. Our intent was to see Camel Rock.

It is a rock formation that actually looks like a camel. It is a geological marvel formed by the melting glaciers as they left Southern Illinois.

The weather was ideal. Southern Illinois was coming off an extended cold and snowy winter. John and I had been cooped up long enough. We were excited, to say the least. This particular outing had been planned several months earlier. We were not sure, though, if the weather would cooperate with our planning. In Southern Illinois, weather not cooperating with one's plans happens frequently.

Fortunately, the weather did cooperate. I could hardly contain my excitement as I rode up to my buddy's driveway and parked Red.

John met me at the door of his house.

I didn't know whether to laugh or cry.

Purple was all I saw. A big splash of purple

A voice from inside the purple invite me in.

I realized it was my riding buddy, John. "He must be playing some kind of trick on me." I thought. We're going riding. Where's his treasured leathers, and, and WHY is he in purple leathers? I can't wait to hear this story!"

Just as I stepped through the door, Doris, John's wife, greeted me with a big wide smile. She seemed especially happy and couldn't wait to let me know why.

"What do you think of John's new riding outfit?" she asked through a broad enthusiastic smile?

I was in serious trouble. That's an extremely unfair, loaded question. How is a man supposed to answer a question like that? Your macho friend is standing next to his new wife and you don't want to hurt either of their feelings. But, purple on a macho guy like John? And his wife of two months wants to know your opinion? The answer you give could be very problematic.

John was a confirmed bachelor until he met Doris. At age fifty, John finally met the love of his life. Doris was twenty four years younger, full of energy, and intent on pleasing her man. They married two months ago after a short but intense courtship.

Fortunately, before I could respond to Doris's question she explained the purple leathers.

"I bought his outfit for his birthday. He complained so much about his other outfit and he never did anything about it, that I just took it as a hint. I went to the Harley store the other day while he was at work and found these. I thought they were pretty and very colorful.

I worry about him being visible on his black motorcycle with his black outfit. The guy at the store said John would have no problems being seen when he wears these. I'm not so sure, though, that John really likes them.

I think he looks sexy! I can't wait to go riding with him.

But this day belongs to you two. John tells me you've been waiting for this ride all winter. So go have fun." She gave her husband a kiss on the cheek and bounced out of the room.

I still didn't know what to say. It was up to my buddy to be the first to say something. But he didn't.

John enjoys his machoism, but purple does nothing to enhance that image. I'm pretty sure he sensed that as well. Doris bought the outfit for him and he absolutely adores his new bride. I'm sure that was enough.

He turned around, walked through the kitchen,

opened the door to his garage, then pushed the button to open his garage door, and went straight to his bike. I followed behind him through the garage and went to my scooter.

He pushed his big ol' Harley out of the garage and went through his pre-ride routine.

John is not necessarily a big talker. He's kind of like Sylvester Stallone and Clint Eastwood. They are men of few words, but when they speak, you listen. John was not speaking.

I watched John stroke his beard and then grab his helmet with his right hand. He put his left hand on his forehead and smoothed back his hair from front to back, just like he always did, before proceeding to put on his helmet. And like always, John took great care his ponytail was just in the right place on his shoulder.

I really wanted to talk about that new set of leathers, but if John wanted to say anything he would.

When he finally mounted his bike and started it up, I about lost it. Fortunately I already had my helmet on and my visor down so he couldn't see me quietly laughing at the site of that Harley dude in purple leathers on that big bike. Believe me, John always took great pride in his biker dude appearance, but I was of the opinion this definitely put a crimp in that appearance.

John was ready, so off we went.

We don't communicate when we ride until we get to a predetermined place.

We generally ride about three hours before we stop to rest. But it did not happen on this day.

John and I had heard that a group of motorcycle riders from California were coming through Southern Illinois and we knew what time they were expected. The talk was that they did not necessarily have a good reputation. Supposedly, local law authorities were on alert.

John, for some strange reason, had a notion they would not mind if we rode a short way with them.

Yea, right! Like, I really believed my scooter would be allowed in with that group.

About an hour into our ride, it seemed to me as if John was riding faster than normal. My scooter and I had no problems keeping up with John, but I was worried that we might miss the biker gang from California.

It was needles worry. From out of nowhere, it seemed, they roared up behind us. I knew my scooter had to be a source of amusement. It was the smallest thing on the road at the time. I was convinced I was sticking out like a sore thumb, and needless to say, I felt a little uncomfortable. That was an unnecessary concern.

We were on a two lane back country road with lots of curves. Obviously, we needed to insure we stayed on our side of the road. From what I could see in my mirror it didn't seem to matter to the gang coming up behind us.

At that time and in my current frame of mind, I was of the opinion that they were riding as if they believed the road belonged to only them and there was something in front of them (me) that didn't belong.

I heard their rpms rev up. I believed they were going to check that "something" out in front of them.

There were six in the group of motorcycle riders. The 1950 and 60's Hell's Angels came to mind.

But they passed me without so much as a look. I noticed the high handle bars on a couple of bikes. All the bikes had lots of chrome and fat tires. Patches covered their well worn black leather jackets. Some of the patches appeared to be of the skull and cross Variety.

They wore big heavy looking black boots. I swear I saw spurs of some sort attached to the boots. One guy was wearing a black half helmet with a spike on top. Every one of them were scary looking characters.

Anyway, they all passed me as if I was a rock in the road they didn't want to run over. The lead guy was pointing at John. He slowed his bike down and looked directly at my buddy. I was worried. The leader sped up and went on by. The second biker took the leader's place next to John, studied him, and then drove on by. Every single guy in that group did the same.

John, as far as I could tell, did his best to be unconcerned about those checking him out. I was worried, though, for John and worried that we may have to also deal with on-coming traffic. A sharp curve was rapidly approaching.

I needlessly worried on both counts. It seems I did a lot of needless worrying that day.

When the last Hell's Angel got by John, they all grouped up in front of us riding side by side. It appeared as if they were discussing something. We watched as they rode into the curve ahead.

John slowed his bike down and pulled it to the side of the road a few yards ahead of the curve. The other motorcycles were now out of sight. He turned his bike around and headed back in the direction we came.

I followed his lead.

About ten minutes later, I saw John look behind me. He slowed his bike again and pulled it into the next farmer's lane. I pulled in behind him.

All he said was "That was scary. Let's head home." I agreed. An hour and a half later we pulled into John's driveway. John parked his bike in the garage. I told him

I'd see him next week-end and then I left.

The total time of this ride was about three hours.

I happened to see John at McDonald's the next day. We talked a little about our ride. He and I were both convinced that the riders we saw the day before didn't really know what to think about the "purple dude" on the Harley and that we were wise to turn around. Perhaps they would have allowed us to ride with them, perhaps not? We will never know.

My Harley riding buddy did tell me he was going to buy another pair of leathers. Doris was OK with it because he told her how much he stood out to the Hell's Angels.

I never did, though, find out what happened to the purple leathers.

Dark and Stormy Night!

Tap, Tap, Tap. Was all I heard; ever so softy at first.

"It's only a dream," I thought. I'll just open my eyes to my familiar bedroom surroundings, then close them and go back to sleep.

I've had bad dreams before. Sometimes I remember them. Sometimes I don't. Lately, though, when the bad dreams come, it seems all I have to do is tell myself to open my eyes and they go away never to return. This time will be no different.

I open my eyes and blink a couple of times. It feels like I am awake, but I'm never sure until I check my surroundings. First I must locate the bedroom door. I sleep on my back so that process is not difficult. It just requires a turn of the head to my left.

Just like all the other times before, subdued darkness engulfs me. Our bedroom is never in complete darkness because the hallway night light slightly illuminates the room. A little light always creeps in, especially since my wife insists we keep the bedroom door open. That subtle lighting makes it easier for me to orient my mind to the surroundings as I wake from one of those dreams.

Once I find the bedroom door, my eyes adjust and my mind starts analyzing the surroundings. First, it locates the bathroom door across the hallway. Then my wife's dresser. Then finally, the window. Once the window is found, the mind usually deems me awake enough to recognize that I am indeed in my own home and no longer in the land of make believe.

But something's different this time. Those noises that woke me haven't stop.

What was I hearing and where are they coming from? I turn to look at my wife. Is she breathing? I can see her chest moving. I take comfort in that.

I don't want to wake her. No sense alarming her now. I roll onto my back and take a deep breath and hold it. I need to be sure it wasn't my own breathing I heard.

Tap, Tap, Tap.

"What is that noise?" I whisper. "It doesn't sound like someone trying to break in. I'll lay here a little longer and try to figure out where it's coming from."

"Sounds like a dog."

"It can't be. Sandy died last year." But yet, I know I heard a dog bark.

My brain always functions at a diminished capacity when awaken unexpectedly in the middle of the night. I take in another breath and hold it. I have to be absolute sure I am hearing those noises and not dreaming them.

TAP! TAP! TAP!

"OK! That's real! I am not dreaming!" I whisper. "I really do have to check it out now."

As quietly as I can, I slide out from between the bed sheets and place first one foot then the other on the floor. I sit on the edge of the bed for awhile to insure my brain can function well enough to handle foot movement.

"Now where'd that noise come from? I'll check the family room. If it is someone trying to break in, it won't be from the front of the house... Too much light."

It's time like this when I appreciate our ranch style house. Not a whole lot of corners to negotiate in the middle of the night when I'm not fully mental. I'll walk down the hallway to the kitchen, turn right, and walk about ten steps to the family room. I can do that in my sleep. No problem.

Walking down the hallway, I hear a different noise. It sounds like someone scratching on a window. It's coming from the family room, I think.

I must be still dreaming. That scratching sounds just like something I'd hear in a scary movie.

As I enter the family room, I can feel my heart beating faster. If this is a dream I'm in, it's about to turn creepier. What am I gonna' see when I look out that window? Will I be staring back at the face of some predator peeking in the window to see if anyone is home? Perhaps it's that Jason character?

I wish my mind wouldn't do that! Especially on missions like this.

Now is the time to really gather up all the courage I can muster.

A flash of light suddenly filled the window pane. My heart jumped into my throat. Was that the face of Jason I saw in that flash of light?

How come I never noticed that lightening before? Come on now, Pete, just because you saw "Friday the 13th" last night doesn't mean Jason is real. This has got to be a dream.

"Get yourself together!"

I press my face against the window pane to get a better look at what's outside. A longer look this time reveals a different eerie scene. The moon is absent in the night sky. The clouds look heavy and ominous. The wind is gusting. The trees appear to be stretching their limbs in a 45 degree angle. I can hear drops of water splatting against the window screen.

The good news is, I saw no Jason, or anything human, animal, or monster looking. It's just a bad storm so, obviously, I'm not dreaming.

Off in the distance, I see a faint lightning bolt.

Suddenly, I hear what sounds like fingernails scraping across a chalkboard.

The thought momentarily crept back in. "Jason!"

Another look; I see the same moonless sky and tree branches still bending in the gusting wind.

I can't see the source of the scratching, though. That means a trip outside to get a closer look.

I grab my raincoat from the closet, find my old pair of slip on shoes, and head out to the back porch and into the chilly air.

There was that scratching sound again... And the tapping... And the sound of a dog barking; more of a whimper, actually.

Without thinking, I search for the spot where I buried our dog. "I buried Sandy out there last year. Is she still in her grave?"

"Chez, Pete! What's the matter with you? I know it's the day after Halloween, but this is stupid."

Another flash of light! A little closer this time. Every hair on my body feels charged with electricity. My body is tingling. Is it from the electrically charged air or from anticipation of what I fear may be coming in the next few seconds.

Another brief splash of light reveals that nothing has changed. There's still no moon. Those clouds are still huge ominous puffs in the sky. The rain drops aren't as big as I thought, though. There're just millions of them hitting the ground. It looks like a lake out there. The rain drops appear to be coming straight down like the blade of a guillotine.

The words, "It was a dark and stormy night" popped into my mind. Is this what the author of those words wants his readers to actually feel?

There are those noises again.

The metal shed, it's in the back yard. That must be the source of the scratchy sound.

Standing on the edge of the porch didn't help me see it. I stick my uncovered head out from under the cover of the porch and look toward the shed.

Another flash of lightening!

Ow! Ow! Ow! Why didn't I think about how much a million drops of rain hitting my head would feel like?

The brief look gives me enough of an opportunity to survey the terrain.

The large oak tree next to the shed is now covering the metal building.

What a relief that is! Now I don't have to deal with it until daylight. Case solved.

But what about that barking dog? Why is it barking?

Reluctantly, I pull my rain coat tighter and head out into the rain. The water from my newly formed lake covers my shoes. My pajama bottoms immediately stick to my legs. The rain pelts my head. It feels like I'm being stung by a swarm of bees. Undaunted, I go on to the sound of the barking dog.

What happens next is totally unexpected and unwanted.

The dog, a stray I've never seen before, works itself free from the fallen branches and scampers off.

One would think I would be happy about that.

Not me. I had risked my life, limb, and the threat of Jason to see what was happening here.

After all I just went through; it would be nice to tell the story of how I heroically rescued a wounded animal in the middle of a dangerous thunderstorm.

Now all I have to look forward to is going back into the house and try to give my wife some plausible story as to why I'm so wet.

    O! How I wish this would have been a dream! It would have been more rewarding.

The Wallet

It was going to be a beautiful September day. The weather predictors said no rain, a light breeze, and low 80's. It was the perfect day for riding. I was scheduled off work and planned to enjoy a ride.

As I was gearing up, the phone rang. I gave some thought to not answering it. After all, in another minute or two I would be gone and unavailable to answer it anyway. But I looked at the caller-ID and saw it was my wife. Of course, I am going to answer that call.

CJ called to tell me she wanted to stay an extra day in St Louis with her friend. The two of them were planning to visit the Arch. I had been trying for years to get her up there. Apparently, her friend had convinced her to make the trek.

My wife was retired, it was Friday, and she would still be home to spend the weekend with me. It told her to have fun.

We had planned to pick up that day a new fancy microwave we ordered a couple weeks earlier. I told CJ that I'd wait until Saturday to pick it up with her.

CJ suggested, since I was home anyway, to go ahead and get it. It would only take about an hour. I'd still have plenty of time to ride, especially since she was not coming home.

I agreed. We said our goodbyes and I got myself ready to make a different trip. If truth be known, I was more anxious than CJ to bring that baby home. I am a kitchen aide appliance geek.

I took off my riding gear, gathered up my car keys, drove to the store, went directly to the customer service counter, and told the lady I was there to pick up my fancy new microwave.

She told me how much I owed. I reached for my wallet... My heart sank!! It was not in my back pocket where I always kept it.

I stepped away from the counter to think.

"Where is it? I must have had it when I got coffee this morning at Hardees. Wait a minute! Bill paid for my coffee. Did I even take my wallet out of my pocket?"

As hard as I tried, I couldn't remember. The only thing I could think of was that I left it at Hardees. I decided to drive there to do some backtracking.

By the time I got back to the restaurant, it would be a couple hours later than when I had breakfast coffee. I was sure this was a futile endeavor. If I did leave it there, I did not have much confidence that I would get it back.

My wallet had a business card in it with my contact information. No one had called me yet. I didn't have much money in it, but I did have a couple of credit cards to be concerned about. One of them I planned to use for the microwave.

I asked the manager if anyone had turned in a wallet. He assured me that no one had, but he would let me know if someone did later. "Fat chance of that happening", I thought. I turned around and headed for the exit.

All I could do now was to get back in my car and go home. So I left the building wondering what I was going to do about my situation.

As I exited the restaurant's door to the parking lot, I saw a dark blob on the ground that could have passed for a wallet. I remembered that I parked my car earlier in the general area of that blob.

My mind focused only on that blob. It was racing with the possibility that the blob really belonged to me.

"Could that really be my wallet?" I thought.

"How could I have not seen it when I entered

Hardees a few minutes ago? I had to walk over it. And how many people and cars passed over that same spot since I left here this morning?"

My brain was telling my eyes to focus harder on the blob on the ground.

"Hallelujah! I think it really is my wallet!!"

My eyes and brain finally took in the entire picture. They were now seeing something extremely disturbing. A giant of a man had just scooped up the wallet. He opened it up and I saw him rifle through it.

"Oh my!!" I thought. "He's huge!"

I took a quick inventory of his stature and judged him to be 6' 8", 350 lbs. or so, all muscle, and very intimidating looking. I imagined him to be a defensive end for the St. Louis Rams.

I fretted. "What am I gonna' do now?

He just picked up my wallet."

I am not a confrontational person, but I was sure that defensive end guy had MY wallet. Right or wrong, perhaps because of my own diminutive stature (I'm 5'6" and 150 lbs), I get defensive about big men like that. I assume they are all aggressive and like to express their authority over all the smaller creatures of the world.

He had my wallet and I had to suck it up and get it from him somehow.

I raised my head skyward so I could look him in the eyes. I walked confidently, but not confrontationally, straight toward him. The closer I got to him the more I had to crane my neck. I could tell he knew I was approaching him. We both knew we were going to enter each other's personal space.

The big man could tell that I was looking at the wallet he held in his hand. The moment of truth had arrived, but I was not yet sure what I was going to do if he would not want to talk about the wallet or give it back.

Because of my frame of mind, I don't think I prepared myself for what happened next.

The big man in a quiet almost soothing voice said, "This must be yours? You look like the picture on the license. I bet you were fretting about this? I know I would be." He handed it to me. I enthusiastically thanked him and he walked on in to Hardees and I walked to my car.

What a nice fellow!

God never misses an opportunity to teach. I believed that confrontation was about to happen. That big guy obviously had no thought about creating a problem. He just wanted to do the right thing. I was the judgmental one.

I got back in my car, thought about God's lesson, headed back to the store, and picked up the microwave. I honestly gave no more thought about how I lost the wallet. It wasn't important. The lesson was.

After arriving home I hooked up the microwave and figured out how to work it. I cooked some lunch in the new appliance, suited back up, and headed out for a short afternoon scooter ride. My wife was going to be home later and I couldn't wait to show her how to use the microwave.

When CJ got home, I very proudly showed her how to use the newest kitchen appliance. Then I told her about the experience with my wallet.

She just looked at me and said "Why do you do that?"

What could I say?

Conflicted

"I hear Ned Buntline wants to put you in one of his books, Sheriff. How do you feel about that?"

"I don't particularly care for it. When he puts you in one of his books, unwanted things happen. And it is what's in those books, you are judged by."

"I don't understand. Don't you want to be famous, like Wild Bill?"

"Nope."

"I don't understand?"

"I am a tough lawman, and do have the real reputation to go with it. It's what I did to earn that reputation. It's not a made up reality some writer created in his own mind to help sell his books."

"Sheriff, you do have a reputation of being a tough but just man. You carry that fancy Colt on your hip, but I've never seen you use it. Yet you are well known around here for your gun abilities. How many gunfights have you been in?"

"It's my reputation that makes not drawing my Colt much easier. I resolve issues without the use of gunplay. Innocent people run the risk of getting hurt whenever a gun is drawn. People believe me to be a superb gun handler. And that's Ok. It helps me keep the peace around here."

"That didn't answer my question, Sheriff. Have you ever been on the street to meet a man face to face in showdown, like those characters in the Western books?"

"Son, perhaps, because of my reputation, I have never had to meet a man, face to face, on the street, in a showdown."

"It's almost Noon. Dirk Jackson's gonna' be out there in the middle of that street in a few minutes. If you've not actually done that before, aren't you worried?"

"I have dealt with bad men before. Jackson read

The Mighty Spartan! And His Common Man Adventures

about himself in one of Buntline's books and is just trying to live up to his expectations. Buntline says he frequently meets the local lawman in the street to duel. Dirk's just some penny ante outlaw that's been luckier than most.

The thing is, though, Ned Buntline makes lots of money creating legends. Facts don't seem to be too important to him. Men met their demise because of Buntline's money making scheme.

I've read some of his novels and met some of his legends. I even incarcerated two or three of them without using my pistol.

Ned Buntline and other dime novel writers are the big problem in the West, not these make believe legends. It's the "code of the west" thing these writers created that puts me on the street today."

"Code of the west? What's that?" "They're just a set of unwritten rules of survival all of the West supposedly lives by. The truth is they don't really exist, except in the minds of these writers from the East."

"With your reputation, how come you're not in one of his books?"

"I met Buntline long before I became a sheriff. He was beginning to create his legends back then and I watched his legends struggle to live up to what they were supposed to be. They had no choice. People believed what was written about them.

Even back then I had a strong sense of right and wrong. My code was and still is the same as the men who wrote the words of the Bible. Those words don't seem to be what men like Buntline feel are words to sell by.

I felt strongly about using those words to help in the development of this new land. I had no desire to be a romanticized character in a dime novel. That would require me to live up to a different set of standards.

The West, in reality, is a hard and often unforgiving land. Most of us are just trying to survive.

Some of us, like the cowboy getting ready to face me now, find it easier or more thrilling to take. That makes him an abuser of God's word. There is nothing romantic about that. I let God guide me."

"SHERIFF, I'M OUT HERE IN THE STREET. YOU KILLED MY BROTHER! IT'S TIME FOR YOU TO MEET YOUR MAKER!"

"It's time, son. It will be over soon."

"Dirk, we don't have to do this."

"YOU KILLED MY BROTHER!"

"It was him or me, Dirk."

"DOESN'T MATTER, YOU KILLED MY BROTHER! IT'S YOUR TURN TO DIE!"

"Dirk, we don't have to do this. There is another way."

"Yep! There is and you're still gonna die!"

I wonder? Will he actually draw his gun against me? Somehow, I know he will. His eyes tell me nothing else. Death is all they see.

He has the reputation that tells me he will.

I feel no evil. I am not afraid of evil.

I will not draw first, but I will defend myself and this land I love.

"SHERIFF, YOU KILLED MY BROTHER!"

His eyes tell me his intentions. I see his hand drop toward his gun.

Time slowed down…

I sense my hand reach for my gun.

His hand is already on the butt of his weapon and

his thumb on the hammer.

I feel the handle of my Colt and my finger on the trigger. My hammer is already cocked.

Jackson's yelling something at me and yanking his gun out of his holster.

The barrel of his gun is already pointed at my chest.

Somehow mine is now pointed at his.

I see him squeeze the trigger, hear the roar of the gun, and see the black powder smoke bellowing from it.

I want to move to the right, but I can't until I fire.

Will it be too late?

I hear my gun respond to my finger. Time slowed down even more.

I see Jackson's bullet coming toward my chest.

I see a bullet leave my gun and its path is true.

I feel the sting of his bullet as it enters my chest. The sheer force of its entry into my body has made me lose my footing.

Jackson is falling toward the ground with a hole in his shirt where his heart would be.

I am convinced he breathes no more.

And, like my adversary, here I am, lying on my back.

I see the sun shining bright in the sky above me.

I'm burning up.

People are gathering around me.

I can't make them out.

I know all is about to turn black, but I hear a soft feminine voice calling my name.

Could it be an Angel I hear?

"*Sheriff, Sheriff,*"

That voice sounds familiar. Could it Be?

"Honey, Honey, wake up! You're having a bad

dream! Wake up Pete"

My eyes pop open and I realize that soft voice I hear is that of my sweet wife.

That old Ned Buntline Dime Novel I found a few days ago, the Clint Eastwood marathon, and that late night meal really did a number on me.

I had been struggling with something job related and those were a nice distraction.

A decision had to be made about a fellow worker. I was battling with its consequence.

When conflicted, I often turn to Grandpa's diary. It helps me find answers. I could easily get lost in his stories of his old Western friends and their struggles.

I did not see it in his words back when I first obtained his diary, but there was a moral to all his stories. He always let God lead him. I had forgotten that.

I did make the right decision. I know Grandpa Bill would be proud of me.

City Lake Revisited

It was Friday afternoon and I couldn't wait. My lovely date and I were going to have a special night together. A celebration, really. We planned a fancy dinner, some dancing, and a late night rendezvous at City Lake.

"Boy, she sure is beautiful!" was all I could think when the red headed beauty reached for my hand as I escorted her to my car. "She will tell me she didn't spend too much time getting ready." I thought. And that may be true? But she really didn't need much help. She would still take my breath away even if she did nothing.

The drive to the restaurant was about five minutes away. It recently opened up and this was the first opportunity for either of us to try it out. The restaurant was supposed to be an upscale place.

The first thing we noticed upon our arrival were the white linen, strategically placed crown folded cloth napkins on each table, and the well-dressed patrons. No one appeared to be wearing ordinary street clothes. A definite indication of "upscale" for these two commoners.

Neither of us is much into "upscale," but this night was no ordinary night. No hamburger patties with special sauce tonight. The linen table clothes and folded napkins were the perfect touch to our special night.

The waitress escorted us to our reserved table for two and was quick to provide us with menus. Fortunately, the menu did not reflect the prices I thought the linen and napkins suggested. Higher than what I thought reasonable prices, would have provided me with the opportunity to complain. It was a special night, though, and complaining was not appropriate.

I guess the unexpected reasonable prices embolden me.

I jokingly told my red head, "Honey, whatever you want, it's on me. I'll worry about how I'll pay for it later."

"Worry about it later" I thought. That didn't sound too good. But we've been together a while now and I was confident my red head knew what I meant.

CJ lovingly patted my hand, looked me in the eyes, and and with her always warm smile said, "I know, Dear. You"ll take good care of me."

We ordered a nice cut of steak, sides, and then treated ourselves to desert. It was undeniably better than the fast food we could have chosen.

After the meal was over, we left a good tip and left the restaurant. I held the door open as she walked through it. She grabbed my hand. The warmness of her hand felt very good and exhilarating. The restaurant was busy so we were not able to park close. It did not matter. It just meant I could enjoy her hand in mine a little longer as we walked back to the car.

With the meal over we now had the opportunity to visit with our friends at the Community Center. The Center was hosting a dance with a live rock-n-roll band. They specialized in 50s and 60s music.

There was no question about it. We were going to have fun.

The parking lot at the Center seemed full. We made a couple laps around it before we found an empty spot in which we could park.

After I parked the car, I looked at my pretty red head and told her not to move. I exited the car, walked around the back, opened her door and offered her my arm which she immediately accepted. My heart momentarily skipped a beat.

We walked arm in arm to the Center. My red head

was just as excited as I was. I could tell. I could feel her heat beating.

Our friends, Dave and Martha, Bobby and Susan, had already reserved a spot for us. It's a blast whenever we get together. Bobby is the only good dancer of the guys. All three of the girls are terrific dancers, though. Dave and I are always up to trying not to trip ourselves or our dates while on the dance floor.

The band was playing all the good songs; fast, slow, and in between. They were playing an Elvis tune, *"Can't Help Falling In Love With You"* when we entered. I thought the song quite appropriate.

We strolled, twisted, watusied. And even did the swim. As always Dave and I can at least say we attempted those dances. It did not matter to me how I looked. I was dancing with my sweetheart.

Slow songs have always been my preference. And this night the band played many. I love dancing with my sweetheart to a slow song?

At eleven, CJ and I said our goodbyes and left the dance. We had other plans at City Lake.

It had been many decades since the first time I actually worked up the nerve to share that location with my red head. As before we left a dance from this very same community center. I had surprised her with a visit to a secret parking place at City Lake.

That night we drove down the tree lined half mile rocky road to my secret spot. A drive that seemed to take forever.

The atmosphere, the quiet, the esthetics, the seclusion, and my plan. It was all there. But our privacy and my plan had been violated by unexpected visitors. We were sure it would be again if we returned. The secret spot was no longer secret. There was no reason,

The Mighty Spartan! And His Common Man Adventures

therefore, to ever try that adventure again.

Until this night! We were sure enough time had passed.

It did not seem as if much had changed at City Lake when we revisited it. Like before the drive down the tree lined rocky road seemed to take forever. Just as it was so many years before, the parking lot was empty. To my surprise, I found the same indentation. A little more grown up, but it was there. My truck would have no problems. I backed into it and turned off the lights.

Just like the last time, the sky was full of stars. Their lights still reflected in the calm water of the lake. The night was quiet. I could almost feel Frankie and Annette again. I pulled up the middle armrest so my date could slide next to me. She did. I put my arm around her shoulders as she placed her head on mine. We sat there quietly and enjoyed the silence. It was magical.

After a few moments we reminisced about how the night ended the last time we were here. My beautiful red head and I were confident this time this night was going to end the way it was intended to end all those years ago.

"Remember the night the last time we were here." I said as I looked into her dreamy eyes. "The sky was full of stars. Just like tonight. And we tried to count them."

I turned away to look out my window. "Nothing's changed." I said and started counting. Soon, I lost my way in the count. The stars disappeared.

When they reappeared I could no longer feel my right arm. I ignored the feeling. It was nice having my red head rest in my arms with her head on shoulder.

Still staring out my window, I broke the quiet of the night and said, "I told you then, Darling, I was hooked on a feeling. I still am."

I turned back to look into the eyes of my beautiful red head. But I couldn't see them. She was sound asleep. There was a smile on her lips.

I kissed her forehead, ever so softly, so I would not wake her. As gently as I could, I lifted her head off my arm and placed it softly back on my shoulder. Then I started the truck, put it into gear, and drove my sleeping red headed wife back to our home.

Our late night rendezvous with a starry night at City Lake was once again interrupted. The plan had been changed, just as it had been forty five years, three children, and four grandchildren ago.

LOVE is GRAND.

Asphalt and Mc Donald's

Since I retired one of the things I thought I would be able to take advantage of was riding my motor scooter more. And I couldn't wait to take her out on the highway for long rides. Just her & I. Now, I know what some of you are thinking, a scooter on the highway. Is he crazy?

For those of you who have the wrong picture, let me clear up the photo. My motor scooter is a Honda Silverwing. It is classified as a Maxi scooter. Red, as I affectionately call her, has 600ccs. The speedometer, has 120mph printed on it. She won't do that, but she will do over 100mph. I know for a fact. Let's just leave it at that. I can take her anywhere a road worthy motorcycle can go and can easily keep up with them. Done it many times. So I am no more crazy than anyone else taking their bike out for highway rides.

Anyway, on this particular day the weatherman was predicting the temperature was going to get to the upper 90's. I left before 9:00 a.m. It was still cool and leaving that early also insured I would be back in time to help my wife with babysitting. The Grandkids were coming later in the day.

We had many fun things planned with them. One was a trip to McDonald's for supper. They don't have one where they live and like most kids, Happy Meals are a particular favorite. My wife and I were looking forward to watching them eat their favorite food.

Red and I were enjoying our morning ride and all was going according to plan until about lunch time. My brain and belly began to argue with each other. That argument became violent as I was riding through a small village in Southern Illinois. The place only had one stop sign.

As I was approaching it, my belly reminded me, "I am extremely hungry, FEED ME!"

My brain Interrupted, "You are only about one hour from home. EAT THERE!"

Going home meant I would continue going straight ahead and have to listen to the argument longer. Eating meant I would have to make a left turn across on-coming traffic. There was a McDonald's in a neighboring town about ten minutes away.

The belly yelled, "CAN'T WAIT 'TILL YOU GET HOME. FEED ME NOW!"

I had to yield to the wishes of my belly. It spoke the loudest.

I turned my blinker on and stopped at the stop sign. Just as soon as I stopped I noticed a pickup truck coming toward me and pulling up to the stop sign. There was no indication, it was turning. That meant I had to cross in front of him to make my turn.

I was first to the stop sign so it was my turn to go. Because I am on two wheels and going through an intersection, I made sure to make eye contact with that driver. I like to make sure the other guy sees me. I was sure he did. So I entered the intersection and began turning Red to the left.

That pick-up began rolling. At first, I thought he was just in a hurry and was rushing me through the intersection. I figured he would wait for me to pass in front of him before proceeding. I was wrong.

It suddenly became quite clear that he either did not actually see me or he was not going to let me pass in front of him. Either way, if we both proceeded on our same course at the same speed something unpleasant was going to happen. More so to me than to him.

I have no idea how it happened, but the next thing I knew, Red and I were on the hard asphalt in the middle of the intersection. The truck went on by. I am sure he had to swerve otherwise he would have run over us. I never saw him again.

Suddenly, there we were. In the middle of the intersection. Laying on the asphalt.

Lots of thoughts went through my mind. "Am I really on the ground? Am I hurt? Did anybody see me take a spill? How embarrassing! Wait a minute! I'm in the middle of the street. I better get out. I'm blocking the intersection. Gotta pick up Red and get to the side of the road."

More thoughts crept in. "You can't leave the scene of an accident. The cops would write me a ticket, if I did. And then I probably couldn't get the insurance to pay for any injuries."

My brain sure does think funny things in times of stress. Reason took hold, fortunately, and reminded me that I was in more danger to myself and others if I stayed where I was. So it really was time to leave the scene.

"Wait a minute. I can't get my leg up! How come? Looks like Red's laying on it."

I honestly was not too concerned at that point. I'd pull my leg out from under the scooter, pick up Red, and go on to the fast food restaurant, a little embarrassed and angry.

But my leg wouldn't move. It was firmly lodged between the back of the scooter and the road. The thought of a broken leg suddenly entered my conscience. "If my leg is broken, how am I going to get to the side of the road? I'd have to push Red from my knees, I guess."

Although it seemed like minutes, only a few seconds had passed since I deposited myself on the road. Apparently, traffic had decided I was not impeding their progress. The car behind me at the stop sign went on by. Red was still laying on her side in the middle of the intersection with my leg pinned underneath her. I actually worried about having to play traffic cop while trying to get to the side of the road.

It became abundantly clear that I was on my own. No one was coming to my rescue.

Fighting embarrassment and disappointment in the lack of human support, I twisted my body around, grabbed the back of the scooter, and hoped I could lift her enough to dislodge my foot. Red weighed over five hundred pounds. Most of her weight was on my foot. And I needed to lift that dead weight while lying on my back. I had a great deal of concern about my ability to lift that much weight, even it was just a few inches. If I couldn't I would have to scream in agony until someone came to my assistance.

Fortunately, I did not have to suffer that humiliation. I managed to lift the scooter enough to pull my foot out. I felt a sharp pain in my ankle as I placed it on the ground and put weight on it while lifting Red to a vertical position.

There were four corners in the intersection. To which corner was I going to push her?

At that point, I didn't much care if traffic had to wait on me or not. I was in a great deal of pain and I was not going to abandon Red. She was coming to the side of the road with me. Traffic would just have to wait or run me over.

Fortunately, they waited. But as soon as I was clear of the street, the traffic went on.

My ankle was killing me but I was not going to lay Red back down on the ground. She had already suffered enough humiliation. There was no sidewalk at the side of the road where I was going, so I had to push her into the grass. I put her kickstand down (and it takes two feet to do so. One to pull the kickstand down, the other to hold the scooter) and gently rested her on the stand. Although it had not rained for awhile, I had to make sure she would not fall over. I slowly but gently, and with additional pressure on my aching foot, lowered Red onto the kickstand.

Knowing she was securely in place, it was time to asses my injuries. I attempted to walk in a normal stride. It became painfully clear that my left foot would not allow normal weight. I thought I must have a severe sprain but convinced myself I would be able to walk it off, eventually.

A couple of boys ten to eleven years of age walked by and asked if I was OK. I told them I was. They were watching me hobble around like a bunny rabbit so I don't think they were convinced. They asked me again and offered to help. I told them once again I would be OK.

Suddenly, I began to feel as if I might possibly throw up.

"This is going to be embarrassing!" I thought. "I'm going to vomit in front of everybody, right here in the middle of town. I'm gonna make a mess. Better find an inconspicuous place."

But there wasn't any. Then I remembered, nobody cared enough to help me out of the street. Why should I care if I make a mess?

False alarm! I didn't throw up. So I sat down on the ground next to Red. It was time to figure out what I was to do.

My belly started yelling again and this time giving conflicting reports. "I'm hungry!" and "You better not feed me. I might throw it up!"

My left foot was also seeking attention. "I'm hurting, you better figure out what's wrong!"

My eyes were searching for someone, anyone, to help me figure out what I was going to do.

I was alone and going to have to work that out on my own. A difficult feat, indeed, considering that my brain had a heightened sense of dullness. A new found concern that there was a possibility I might pass out right there on the side of the road had presented itself shortly after I sat down.

But, from somewhere in my confused brain, a thought had found its way. "Call Dr. Mom! She'll know what to do."

"That's fine and dandy," I thought, "but where the heck is my phone?"

After padding me down, I realized it was in Red's glove box. Fortunately, that box was an arm's reach away. After grabbing the cell phone, I speed dialed my wife.

In retrospect I was most likely near stroking, so I can't be sure. I think the conversation went something like this:

"Hi Babe. How're you doing?"

"I'm in DeSoto and I got some bad news."

"You wrecked your scooter, didn't you? Are you OK?" My wife sure was perceptive.

"I think so. I'm hungry, my foot hurts, I'm sittin' on the side of the road." That was certainly a peculiar way to describe my situation.

CJ knows me well. From those few words she was able to assess my state of affairs.

"Forget about eating and call 911!"

I protested. I insisted on getting back on my scooter, ride to the fast food joint, and then check myself into our local emergency room.

Using her powers of gentle persuasion, my loving wife told me to go ahead and do what I wanted. "But," she said, "If you get back on your scooter and try to ride to the restaurant, you will be scraped up off the asphalt. Don't expect me to come visit you in whatever hospital you end up in!"

She didn't mean it, of course. But she was concerned that I would indeed try to go eat before taking care of any necessary medical needs. Up until my wife chastised me, I was giving strong consideration to eating first. She knows me so well.

Just as I was promising her I would call 9-1-1, an ambulance and a police officer drove up. I informed CJ that 9-1-1 had just arrived somehow and I would talk to her later when I knew more. Boy, was I thankful for their arrival! I would no longer have to endure my wife's appropriate chastisement. Those young boys must have told someone to make the call.

The paramedics assessed my condition. They were going to load me up in the ambulance and take me to the emergency room in Carbondale, IL. Of course, I made sure that didn't happen until the police officer assured me Red would be protected until I could pick her up in a day or two.

For the first time ever, I got to see what the inside of an ambulance looks like and what it is like to ride in one. I was a little bummed out, though. It was a slow ride to the hospital. I was really hoping for a speedy trip with the sirens blaring. O Well!

The doctors determined my ankle was broken and would most likely be in a cast for a while.

My wife was not be happy about that because we were leaving for Germany in a couple of weeks to see our son. A broken ankle might jeopardize the trip. It didn't, fortunately. But that is another story.

Red was OK. She wound up with only very minor scratches.

Red and I had managed to rearrange my wife's day. She was babysitting our Grandchildren and enjoying their company. Because of my mishap, CJ had to load them up in her car, drive them to a hospital sixty miles away so that she could pick up PaPa from the emergency room.

After being released from the hospital I told CJ I was hungry. Imagine that? I hadn't eaten since breakfast.

My loving wife loaded up her ailing husband and her Grandchildren and headed to the very same McDonald's I tried to eat at hours earlier. So as it turned out, I was able to treat my Grandchildren to Happy Meals after all.

By day's end, all was right with the world. At least my Grandchildren thought so. They got their Happy Meals and got to help PaPa in and out of the car.

Magazine Land U.S.A

When I was growing up, Sparta had two very prominent industries. They were coal mining and printing. Both provided a good standard of living for its workers.

We had teachers, doctors, lawyers, businessmen, and such. Every town does. But in a town of three thousand five hundred people the largest percentage of them worked either in a nearby coal mine or in our printing plant.

Most of the adults I knew who didn't work "Downtown" or in a mine were associated in some way with World Color Press. Everyone in town referred to it as the "Comic Book Factory."

Nearly one third of our population was employed by the factory. Many types of magazines were printed there. If you bought the TV guide or a popular comic book, most likely, it was printed in Sparta.

My dad took great pride in telling me the comic book factory was started by actress, Betty Grable's, grandfather. I think that is true, but I am not positive.

Having connections to a famous movie star was neat. My Dad told me she was a big Hollywood star. The word Hollywood was enough for me.

Betty Grable was a huge star in the 1940s. I am pretty sure I had never seen any of her movies. I believed her movies were primarily romantic. Yuk! Not the type of movie I watched as a child.

That didn't make any difference to me. My Dad used the word "Hollywood." That, of course meant she must have known the likes of Clark Gable, John Wayne, Gary Cooper, and maybe even Roy Rogers. In my youthful mind, I thought that if, indeed, Betty Grable did know those great actors there was a possibility that one of them might show up in Sparta. Especially

The Mighty Spartan! And His Common Man Adventures

since we had a connection to Hollywood through the grandfather of a famous star. Hey! I was a kid. What would I know about how things really worked?

I was raised in Sparta during the Golden Age of Comics. Many of my favorite comic book characters had their adventures printed right here in good o' Sparta, Illinois, the comic book factory of the entire world.

It was easy for me to imagine seeing Superman flying over our sky while on his way to defeat a villain. Perhaps I'd see The Flash speeding around our streets. Or maybe I'd take comfort in knowing Batman was facing down the Joker.

AAh! Life was great. All that excitement and my little town was part of it.

Now here is some technical stuff about how Sparta printed all those magazines. I am not very technical nor did I ever work there so here is my best explanation of Sparta's printing world.

The Comic Book Factory had the distinction of being the single largest producer of its product in the world. Our factory was instrumental in the creation of a new art form, the Comic Book.

World Color Press began in 1903 when the owners of the St. Louis Star decided they needed a way to handle the additional printing generated by the color printing needs for the Louisiana Purchase Exhibition at the 1904 St. Louis World's Fair. The intent was to shut down the operation after the World's Fair but they decided instead to focus on a new feature. It was the color "funnies" section of the Sunday newspaper.

The Sunday "funnies" became so popular that in order to accommodate the needs and make a profit the "funnies" had to be reprinted in a magazine format. Thus the prototype for the very first comic book.

By the close of World War II, this new form of reading material became the most popular form of newsstand material on the market. By 1948 the demand became so great that a new state-of-the-art plant was built in Sparta, Illinois. Within five years, World Color Press became the largest producers of comic magazines in the industry. A title they held into the 1990's.

The Comic Book Factory had massive offset presses. Huge rolls of paper were fed through them like ribbon on a spool. These letterpresses could produce tens of thousands of impressions an hour. Those presses could print two 32 page comics at a time and produce up to 15,000 copies an hour.

By the 1970s the operation became so huge that the Comic Book Factory purchased more equipment and expanded their plants into other communities. Sparta, consequently, became known as "Magazineland U.S.A."

All those comics had places to go and people to read them. A means of moving them out of town had to be established. So distribution centers were set up. From these centers the comic magazines would be loaded up in trucks and sent all over the country. This massive effort took hundreds of people to make it happen.

In its heyday our Comic Book Factory employed as many as one thousand people. Including those employed by the distribution centers nearly one thousand five hundred people were provided good paying jobs by the printing industry.

Unfortunately, the comic book factory did not survive modern day warfare. The printed word, in today's world, does not have the same influence as it once did. With the advent of the personal home computer, we now live in a digital world. The need for the printed word had been drastically reduced. Thus the demise of our printing plant.

The world around my little community changed and constantly presented it with many difficult challenges. But unlike the comic book factory, Sparta survived and thrives.

*Sparta, Illinois USA
(My hometown)*

I am glad I was able to fight my way back home to Sparta. It's a neat little town.

Geography will tell you that we are located in the United States of America, in the state of Illinois, and the county of Randolph. We are about sixty mile East of St. Louis, Missouri. According to the 2010 census, the population is about 4300.

In sixty years I have lived in all sizes of communities and even had some extended vacations in foreign countries. I can tell you for a certainty, as far as I am concerned, my small Southern Illinois town is where my final resting place will be. This little town of Sparta offers all I care to have.

I am not comfortable being around large masses of humanity. That lifestyle is, to me, stressful and fast paced. Yes, the city offers much. There are more opportunities for entertainment, employment, and housing. I don't deny that's a good thing.

But small town living has definite advantages. For me it's peace, quiet, and the ability to stretch out my arms. I like feeling OK to sit on my front porch and know I won't hear my neighbor flush his commode. I like not having to drive far to see corn fields.

I don't have to have my mind rushing to make a decision on how soon to move to the next traffic lane. I don't have to worry about the ten cars in front of me, beside me, and behind me. That is more stress than I care to live out the rest of my days with.

Sparta is a community with a rich history. Part of that history includes helping to shape the air industry. Our own legendary Hunter brothers were pioneers in aviation.

My parents used to tell me stories about them. Supposedly they were a little on the wild side. A little would be an exaggeration. The brothers were avid motorcycle riders in their early days and would often perform stunts on them around town.

One day, they rode to St. Louis to trade them in on new ones. They rode by what is now Lambert International Airport and saw several biplanes parked on the airfield. After inquiring about them, the Hunter brothers decided they wanted to learn to fly.

One of the brothers took ninety minutes of flight instruction. The brothers decided to purchase a plane and one of them flew it home. The residents of Sparta were then treated to a constant barrage of stunt flying. Eventually they became proficient enough to establish a flight endurance record on July 4, 1930 of 553 hours, 41 minutes and 30 seconds.

Besides setting some early aviation records, they knew and flew their own planes with many of the early famous airplane pilots. Our own Hunter Field is named after them.

Coal mining has been around in Sparta for almost as long as the town itself. If you were a coal miner, you either worked underground or in a strip mine.

At the beginning of this century, though, coal mining was nearly lost by environmental restriction placed on coal productions. Many miners lost their jobs.

Our coal has a high sulfur content. The restrictions meant our coal had to be cleaned before it could be shipped. Scrubbers, to clean the coal, had to be put in place. To put those scrubbers in our existing mines was extremely costly.

The coal in the Western United States had a much lesser concentration of sulfur. The industry big shots deemed it more profitable to move their emphasis out West. As a result, many of our mines were shut down.

I never work in a mine but I have friends who still do. They told me Western coal was indeed cleaner and that was why the industry moved West. The Western coal, though, was less compact and did not burn as long. Therefore more coal had to be burned.

It seemed, I guess, those buying coal had to buy more and got less value for it. Spending more and getting less doesn't make much sense to me. Eventually, restrictions were eased and technology improved. Coal production has returned to Southern Illinois.

Nearly one third of Sparta's population, while I was growing up, was employed by the "Comic Book Factory." I had many friends employed there. I read a great deal of comic books. Why not, they were free? My friends always seemed to have a supply.

I believe that factory was responsible for many a high school kid driving around town in the "Muscle Cars" of the 60's. Unfortunately, the people dependent upon this industry for income were forced to find it elsewhere. As I stated before, our printing industry did not survive.

With the disappearance of the printing industry and the uncertainty of coal mining future, Sparta could have been in danger of dying like many small towns in America today. Either of those were severe enough to dampen spirits.

For obvious reasons, many of our citizens found employment elsewhere. We turned into a community where people slept in town and travelled out of town to work. Consequently less money was spent in town. Restaurants no longer served as many lunches. Many workers got home after stores closed forcing them to buy out of town.

Revenue decreased.

But my town is resilient and always looking for ways to keep it alive. One such way was to bid for and win the opportunity to host a yearly international event.

Each year Sparta hosts the ATA Grand American shooting competitions with over thirty thousand people in attendance. It is a once a year month long event for youth and adult amateur shooters sponsored by the ATA (Amatuer Trapshooting Association). The event is held at the World Shooting and Recreational Complex in Sparta, Illinois.

The Complex is a state of the art shooting facility with 120 trap fields spread out over three and a half miles. It is also the site of the largest campground in Illinois with one thousand campsites available. The Complex sits on one thousand six hundred acres of reclaimed coal mining land.

The facility not only host shooting events but also hosts a variety of conferences and some outdoor concerts. Charlie Daniels, Willie Nelson, Tim McGraw, and Joan Jett and other notable musicians had concerts in Sparta, Il. The shooters and their families, the conventions, and the concert goers all spend money. That is a big boost to our economy.

If I ever feel the need for the hustle and bustle of "Big City." I get in my car and drive about forty or fifty minutes in any direction and experience it. St. Louis, Belleville, and Carbondale/ Marion area can take care of that need. In fact, my wife and I often end up in one of those areas on our weekly Saturday date night.

We enjoy the experience for a few hours. But we can't wait to get back home and unwind.

I believe anyone who prefers the life of small town USA can probably relate to much of that.

So why is Sparta, Illinois so special to me?

Loyalty and values, I guess. My parents chose to live here and raise their family. Even as a child growing up here, I felt as if the community was looking out for my well-being. Disappointing my family also meant disappointing the community.

Growing up, I watched the town every night on television when I sat down with my family to watch Andy Griffith. Some of Opie's adventures could have been mine. Andy and my Mom and Dad had many things in common.

It appeared to me back then that every adult worked. I doubt if that was true, though. Kids don't really pay attention to that sort of thing. Or at least I didn't.

The citizens of Sparta, Illinois enjoy life in a small town and value family and friends. We look for the positive in life, help each other out and go to church together.

We have what many would call Mid-western core values. We are a small town in Southern Illinois but are proud to also be called Americans. We proudly fly our national flag, honor our soldiers, and pay respect to those who have fallen in battle to protect our God given rights.

We pray to Jesus but respect the rights of others to not do so. We are a hard-working, caring, family centered people.

Life took me away from my hometown for about twenty years. There were times, while I was away, I wondered how my home town would get through the difficult times it was facing. Yet, I had confidence it would.

While I was away, my home town not only met the challenges of losing key industry but I discovered it had significantly increased its population. A feat, I'm sure, would not have been accomplished without engaging in battle.

Throughout the years, Sparta has had many fiscal concerns which threatened possible devastation. Rather than giving up, my community always finds a way to conquer the things that try to suppress it.

I have always and will forever appreciate my hometown's fighting spirit. I am truly convinced Spartans will never give up.

It was Sparta and its small town values that helped make me. Life happens, though, and sometimes, because of it, my small town values are subject to challenges.

Like my home town, I meet those challenges with my sword and shield. I do not, nor will I ever yield; for I am **THE MIGHTY SPARTAN**.

Edmond P. DeRousse

Other Pete Russey adventures can be found in my

Common Man Adventure Series

Edmond P. DeRousse
Author

www.commonmanadventures.com

CPSIA information can be obtained
at www.ICGtesting.com
Printed in the USA
FFOW03n2026130118
44362216-44050FF